BURN EVERYTHING...
THEN FORGET IT

ALSO BY BOSTON TERAN

God Is a Bullet

Never Count Out the Dead

The Prince of Deadly Weapons

Trois Femmes

Giv—The Story of a Dog and America

The Creed of Violence

Gardens of Grief

The World Eve Left Us

The Country I Lived In

The Cloud and the Fire

By Your Deeds

A Child Went Forth

How Beautiful They Were

Big Island L.A.

The White Country

BURN EVERYTHING... THEN FORGET IT

BOSTON TERAN

HIGH TOP PUBLISHING LLC

ISBN: 978-1-56703-018-1

Published in the United States by High Top Publications LLC, Los Angeles, CA and simultaneously in Canada by High Top Publications LLC.

Interior design by Alan Barnett
Cover design and illustration by Boris Cvetkovic

Printed in the United States of America

To Crache 777
. . . You were and are God's number
. . . So, watch over us, friend
. . . As we'll all be along in time

ACKNOWLEDGMENTS

To Deirdre Stephanie and the late, great Brutarian...to G.G and L.S... Miz El and Roxomania...the kids...Melissa Brandzel...Charlene Crandall, for her brains and loyalty...the Drakes at Wildbound... And finally, to my steadfast friend and ally, and a master at navigating the madness, Donald V. Allen.

IT'S A BEAUTIFUL DAY
1965

CHAPTER 1

In August of 1965 a car bomb went off in the parking lot of a Bronx diner. Debris rained down all across the front of that eatery.

Among the falling debris were snapshots, hundreds of them. One of the many was of an abandoned apartment building up around 116th Street.

The abandoned building was covered with graffiti, much of it political in nature. After all, this was the era of the Voting Rights Act and an escalating war in southeast Asia. It was also the time of social insurrection.

The snapshot in question featured this written on the building in red paint:

America v. America
Outcome Uncertain

CHAPTER 2

Bill Castle had pulled into the diner lot. With him were Viola Dash and their attorney and advisor, Gardner Flynn. They had been asked to meet with homicide investigators to see what pertinent information they might have regarding a series of slayings that could have been politically motivated.

They had time before the meeting and stopped at the diner. They had just gotten out of the car when Bill realized he had left his Kools on the dashboard.

"Wait up, I forgot my cigs," said Bill.

While he turned back to get them, the other two waited. A pickup truck loaded down with junk went past. A woman could be seen near the car walking quickly. Viola told Gardner, "It's a beautiful day… too beautiful for where we're going."

A moment later there was the explosion.

ONE STOP TOO LATE 1957

CHAPTER 3

The Bronx was basically Caucasian in 1950. By 1960, there was a surging influx of Puerto Ricans. The Bronx had already started to show decay. White flight, they called it. Racism was more accurate. Federal housing projects like Lincoln Center razed black and Puerto Rican neighborhoods with promises of a new life. Apartments with heat, apartments with protected rents. These promises were sewer bound as soon as they were spoken.

The year was 1957. Billy Castle was ten years old. He was on the IRT train with his mother. They were one stop from the White

Plains Road and Pelham Parkway station when a voice said, "Hey, spic... turn that fuckin' radio off."

It turns out they were one stop too late. And it would be that way forever.

CHAPTER 4

Billy was sitting next to his mother. He had his transistor tuned into WABC playing the hits of the day. Maybe you remember, maybe you heard them on a jukebox sometime... Chuck Berry... the Platters... Little Frankie Lymon and the Teenagers... "Why Do Fools Fall in Love." Music and the prattling of train cars on the elevated. A mix that if you lived it, you didn't forget it.

Even his mother knew the music. Could groove to it. After all she was only twenty eight years old. Practically a kid herself.

The voice came down on both of them now.

"You hear me, spic... Turn off that radio."

CHAPTER 5

It was a hot Bronx afternoon, the hazy light slanting through the steel girders that supported the elevated station along White Plains Road casting shadows across the back of the man staring down at mother and son.

He was a skanky looking piece of humanity. Small, favoring sunglasses you get from an Orchard Beach vendor.

His voice rose dramatically. "Turn it off, fucker."

There were about half a dozen people spread across the train car and not a one wanted any piece of this and they went to staring anywhere but the far end of the car.

His hand was at his side, and in that hand was a knife. A pawn shop stiletto with a chipped dragon handle that Billy's mother saw.

"Turn off the radio, son."

She said nothing about the knife. She stretched out an arm and covered her boy's chest and he understood there was danger.

"We don't want trouble," she said.

Billy turned off the radio and as he did he saw the knife, and the man said to Billy's mother, "But I do."

CHAPTER 6

It took one unreasoned moment for the blade to cut short a lifetime as Billy's mother cried out and grabbed her chest.

The boy came up out of his seat and into the heart of such savagery and hit the man across the side of his head with the transistor radio.

The assailant staggered back and the panicked passengers were up and out of their seats and crowding toward the far end of the car. Billy's mother had slumped over, gasping, then slid to the filthy subway car floor, trying to reach for her son.

Billy hit the assailant across the face with the radio and the knife blade tore open his arm and he hit the man desperately over and over again and the volume on the radio triggered and music flooded the car as the Express came to a screeching halt pulling into the Pelham Parkway station platform.

When the Express came to its stop and the doors opened the waiting passengers were treated to a bloody nightmare and a man threatening the crowd with his knife, and down the stairs he bounded, ranting like some demented avatar, only to disappear into a world of crowded sidewalks and endless traffic.

CHAPTER 7

Warsh lived about five blocks from the station on Matthews Avenue. He owned a small, two family house just up from the Esplanade. A blocky and faceless brick affair he was proud to call his own. Billy's mother was his younger sister. She and the boy lived in the downstairs apartment, he in the upstairs.

Warsh was part owner of a gas station one short block up from the Pelham Parkway elevated. Close enough that with all the traffic and street noise he could still hear people shouting.

He could see a crowd on the platform. And why the Express was not moving. The people on the platform were in a state of panic. A police siren and ambulance began to fill in the blanks.

Warsh was thinking suicide or accident, maybe the untimely heart attack, until some rumpled and distraught housewife with a stroller was telling everyone she passed... "There's been a murder on the train."

THE VIEWING

CHAPTER 8

The murder of Mary Buergos was headlined in the *Riverdale Press* and *Bronx News Press*. They actually identified Mary by her married name, though she was long since divorced and went by her birth name of Warsh.

As for the boy's father—he had split for points unknown before the kid was hatched. Rumor had it he'd gone home to Puerto Rico to hook up with his brother. But every attempt to locate them was a dead end.

CHAPTER 9

The viewing took place at Cooke's Funeral Home on 190th Street, just under the shadow of the elevated. Billy's mother had a lot of friends in the neighborhood and the room overflowed with grief. People whispered among themselves about what the assailant had said. Half the people there were Puerto Rican and well understood what the slur meant and where it would take you.

Billy was there, of course. But he wasn't really. He drifted between a numb despondency and rushes of rage. He couldn't look at his mother, lying there in her lilac blue wedding dress. More girl than woman. He stood beside his uncle, who could not control his crying. In a wracked voice he whispered, "I practically raised her."

When it was time to close the casket and people made their final goodbyes, Billy could not bring himself to kiss her waxlike face. It was not her, not the life that oversaw his own. It was just a figurine now. That reality would haunt him for years.

When he was finally in the room alone with the body he kept staring at a crucifix on the wall above the casket. When the Express passed overhead on the elevated, the cross would tremor.

VIOLA DASH

CHAPTER 10

Viola Dash was sitting on the front steps of the family house in Riverdale. She was listening to WMCA on her transistor and reading *The Adventures of Tom Sawyer* for a class report.

Her father leaned out an upstairs window. "You want to lower that goddamn thing? You can hear it all the way down the block."

She didn't even bother to look up to acknowledge him. She just kept reading and lowered the volume dial a smidge.

He saw what she did.

"Are you fucking with me?" he said.

She kept reading. She lowered the volume another smidge.

"I'm being played by an eleven year old. Lower it or when I get downstairs you lose it."

She kept on reading but she lowered it.

He came out of the house a couple of minutes later and slammed the door behind him.

Charlie Dash was a no nonsense former Marine who still favored a crewcut. He wore expensive clothes, but tasteless. A pure smart ass personality, and proud of it.

"Get in the car, troublemaker."

Viola did as ordered. A book in one hand, radio in the other. Reading the whole time as she climbed into the shotgun seat. Her father climbed into their powder blue Continental.

Charlie had to reach across her to open the glove compartment. From it he took out a revolver which he slipped into his coat pocket. Then to his daughter he said, "Turn off that spook music."

CHAPTER 11

Billy was in the driveway of his house slinging a Spalding Hi-Bounce against the garage door and grabbing it out of the air as it came whooshing back.

His friends called to him from up on the Esplanade that they were heading over to Fordham Road and did he want to come along and wreak a little havoc. But he was too down, too sad, under the influence of too much grief, so he waved them off.

Not much later he was staring up at the upstairs living room window where there were about a dozen lit mourning candles.

He closed his eyes and tried to hear his mother's voice. To imagine her there calling to him. But the ghost can't be caught, and right then a car horn was behind him.

He spun around and there was Charlie Dash in that beautiful baby blue Lincoln.

Charlie pulled into the driveway and parked. He got out of the Continental.

"Hello, Mister Dash," said Billy.

"How you doing, boy?"

Billy shrugged.

Charlie told his daughter, "You stay in the car." Then to the boy he said, "That's my daughter, Viola… I don't know if you ever remember meeting her. She's a troublemaker, Billy, so watch out."

CHAPTER 12

When it was just the two of them, things got quiet. He took to staring at the Spalding he held in his hand. They were just kids who had that moment dropped on them. Billy kept himself at a distance. Viola watched him carefully. It was she who finally spoke.

"My father told me what happened."

"Yeah…," said the boy. "It was pretty bad."

He bounced the ball hard, caught it on the up.

"I saw it too in one of the papers," said Viola.

The boy looked at the house. At the upstairs window.

The Express came rushing past the Esplanade. The fucking sound shot up the back of his neck and there he was in that funeral home inside his head where he could see on the wall that trembling crucifix.

"Where do you go to school?" said Viola.

"Saint Clare's on Hone Avenue."

"Like it?"

"What's to like? The nuns are shit."

He bounced the ball and caught it fast again on the up. He felt he should say something.

"Where do you go?"

"Rye Country Day School."

"I hear that place is—"

"Don't say it. 'Cause I'm gonna be stuck there—"

He grinned slightly. She picked up on it. She was running her fingers over the top of the pages of the Tom Sawyer paperback. A moody silence crept in.

She pointed at his bandaged arm. "Is that from—?"

"Yeah. Twenty two stitches."

"That many," she said.

He looked at the arm like the bandage was a badge of honor or courage. He drifted toward the car, and her. "This is some car," he said.

It was. Beautiful leather upholstery that matched the paint job. And that stylish chrome.

"Elegant," he said.

"Yeah," she said. "And flashy."

He nodded in complete agreement.

"My father is big on flashy," she said. "You want to check it out?" She pointed to the driver's seat.

Talk about a wild fantasy. He was starting around the car when he thought the better of it. He glanced at the house. "I don't know. I don't want to—"

"What are you doing? Go on," she said. "My father won't mind. Really. He's good that way." Then she whispered, "Sometimes."

CHAPTER 13

Whether he heard her as he was climbing into the driver's seat—who knows.

He sat back, hands on the steering wheel like some bigtime showboat, but Viola saw his feet didn't quite hit the pedals and she explained there was an electrical power seat switch and when he got it working that seat moved forward like it was a magic carpet.

His fingers worked those cool chrome nobs and dials. "Ohhhh," he said.

"It's like something out of a movie," said Viola.

"I wish I had a picture of me right now," he said.

Then he realized he was having a moment. A real moment where the dark reality of a dead mother had disappeared. He was just a kid now having a good time when a wave of guilt washed over him that he shouldn't be enjoying himself so much with a dead mother resting against his heart.

Viola picked up the sudden suffering that was spread across the boy's face. She was sensitive to it as she had seen that same look on her father's face, especially when he talked about her mother.

"My mother's dead too," she said.

He looked at her, surprised.

"Leukemia... Two years ago."

He sat there in despair holding the steering wheel.

"I heard that your father was Puerto Rican," she said.

"Yeah," said Billy.

"I'm Puerto Rican," said Viola. "At least that's what they told me."

"What do you mean… what they told you?"

"I was adopted. My parents got me from a foundling in Puerto Rico."

"That's tough."

She shrugged. Then she held up an arm and put it alongside her face. "Do I look Puerto Rican?"

She had short dark curly hair and black full eyebrows and creamy skin.

"Some Puerto Ricans look white, some black, some Spanish," she said.

It was as if he had not heard a word she said. She saw he was far away. His eyes were watering up. He was going to cry and she didn't know what to do about that.

She pointed to a raindrop size cut on his cheek.

"Is that from—"

He nodded.

A silence fell about the inside of the car. They could hear kids now playing in the empty lot next to the house. A roadster shot-gunned by with radio full throttle. Billy looked away from Viola because he was fighting off tears.

She saw and wanted to say something, do something.

She put two of her fingers together and kissed them. He caught this out of the corner of his eye and then she took those two fingers and touched that raindrop wound gently.

He didn't understand. Still looking away, he said, "What did you do that for?"

"Didn't your mother ever do that? Mine did."

CHAPTER 14

It was not just Viola Dash who was a foundling. They were all foundlings in a way, on the doorstep of some unknown future, at the will of some unspoken fate. With a pound of promise the infant that is all of us faces a mountain's worth of pain. We are in a trial—born of untold grace struggling against tragic human folly as we wait to be adopted into the vast amalgam that is America.

AKWESASNE

CHAPTER 15

Warsh closed the living room blinds so the two men could be sure of privacy.

"Police come up with anything so far?" said Charlie.

Warsh went to the breakfront in the dining room and took a mimeograph of the suspect from a stack of copies and handed it to Charlie.

"He looks like a nothing," said Charlie.

"That nothing killed my sister and almost did in my—"

"I didn't mean it like that," said Charlie.

"Sorry, forget it," said Warsh. "I'm just a bundle of bad thoughts. You want something to drink?"

Charlie shook his head no. Warsh poured a drink from a bottle of vermouth and a glass on that breakfront as Charlie lit a cigarette.

Charlie stared at the framed picture on the breakfront that he'd seen endless times over the years. It was he and Warsh from their Marine days when they stormed the beaches at Anzio and marched north to Berlin, leaving a trail of savagery, courtesy of the free world.

Warsh saw what he was checking out.

"It ain't the old days, is it?" said Warsh.

"What we did," said Charlie, "is swap killing krauts and guineas for communists… Light skinned, dark skinned."

Warsh downed a shot of vermouth. "What do you have for me?"

Charlie took a map from his coat pocket along with a page of legal paper and set them on the table. Warsh recognized the map.

"Franklin County again."

Charlie nodded.

Franklin County was in northern New York and flanked the border with Canada. It was also home of the Mohawk Indian Reservation, which had direct access to the border.

A number of places had been marked off on the map.

"Akwesasne," said Warsh.

"Yeah." Charlie pointed to the page of legal paper. "You'll take the bus to Akwesasne. The man I noted there will pick you up. Other names are in case there's… issues."

While Warsh was going over the map and notes, Charlie took the revolver from his pocket that had been in the glove compartment. He set it on the map.

Warsh looked at the weapon, and then at Charlie.

"Not traceable," said Charlie.

CHAPTER 16

Warsh took the Greyhound Express for the four hundred mile trip north to Akwesasne. Warsh had to leave Billy somewhere and pleaded Charlie into doing him a favor. Charlie agreed but Warsh saw he was not hip to the idea, him not wanting any of the poison of the murder to affect his daughter.

The bus depot in Akwesasne was little more than a clapboard building on a block long strip of clapboard and cinder block buildings. The place was textbook rural America just off the Saint Regis River and the huge hydropower dam they were building there.

It wasn't exactly the quiet lazy scene Warsh expected. About a half dozen Mohawk Indians were gathered up around their cars at the end of the street. Some were handing out mimeographs to anyone who passed. They'd even set up a billboard of sorts that read—GIVE US OUR ANCESTRAL LANDS BACK.

What they got were drivers giving them the finger as they sped past.

"Land of the free and home of the brave."

Warsh turned to see who spoke. A young man in a white shirt and tie put out a hand. He was lean and dark, with a real Charles Starkweather face. He wasn't the white shirt and tie type, to Warsh.

"Nick Hargrove," he said. "I sure hope you're the fella I'm waiting for."

"I'm the fella you're waiting for."

"My car's over here."

He was driving an inconspicuous old Plymouth. Hargrove pulled out into the street and started up the highway.

"What's that all about?"

"You mean that little war party? The power dam on the Saint Regis. Rising water level has been sinking a little of the land… They're out to turn back the hands of time… Make waves… They got a hand out for a tasty settlement. We have crews out there fucking with them…." He winked. "A little disruption goes a long way."

Warsh kept tightlipped. He didn't want anything to do with this.

"How was your ride up here? Duller than dirt, probably. At least you're not stuck up here in Deadtown."

CHAPTER 17

Nick drove them out Route 37 toward Bombay. It was all wooded roadsides and long flats of open ground. The rare car or truck sped past, the occasional house in a quiet and still landscape.

"We're in reservation country now," said Nick.

Warsh nodded.

"But you probably knew that."

Warsh nodded again.

"It's best we kept our eyes out for smoke signals."

He laughed at his own wisecrack, but got nothing from Warsh.

"You don't talk much, do you?" said Nick.

"It's best that way," said Warsh.

"Yeah… you're probably right."

He drove on.

They passed a kid and his dog in an open field. The kid would launch a rubber ball and the dog would chase it into the high grass and retrieve it.

Warsh thought about his nephew. The world of that kid and dog were gone to one Billy Castle. It was the world of innocence that was gone to him. Billy Castle, aka Billy Warsh, was now in the shadow of a deadly predator. And the predator was the world.

The boy, thought Warsh, had experienced violence as close up as most soldiers in the war.

The car slowed.

"We're here," said Nick.

He turned onto a dirt road where there was a mailbox on a post. It was a rickety affair. The road made its long and slightly winding way through the dense woods. They drove about half a mile before a farmhouse appeared through streams of light.

A moving van, a twenty footer by Warsh's estimate, was parked alongside a shed. As they passed the house Nick waved and Warsh caught sight of a man watching from a window. He looked to be carrying a shotgun.

They parked and got out of the car. Hargrove unlocked the back of the truck and handed Warsh a flashlight. He also gave him a list of the munitions so he could check that the load was complete. And while Warsh was taking care of all that, Hargrove forewarned him, "I'm waiting on clearance to investigate alternate routes for bringing the weapons across the border, still using the reservation as the point of entry, but setting up backup safe houses."

"What is it?" said Warsh.

"Too much politics with the dam… Too many outsiders… Reporters… Fuckin' left-wing protestors… People wandering up the road, so to speak. Sending all these weapons to Guatemala," said Hargrove. "We'd be better served using them right here."

CHAPTER 18

Warsh pulled up to a warehouse in Brooklyn. It was over on 23rd Street in the Sunset Park neighborhood, and within sight of the piers.

He buzzed the street entry where he had to present his papers and identification. When the rollup door lifted two men took control of the truck and the paperwork. A third man motioned for Warsh to follow him. Everything was so matter of fact. They passed through a half block where slabs of beef hung on great hooks. There were droppings of blood on the concrete floor. Warsh was then led down a drab hallway to an office.

A young man in a well appointed suit glanced up from his paperwork. To Warsh he looked like a college frat boy. His name was Malone.

"You recognize me?" Malone said.

"Generally I make a habit not to recognize anyone… But I make exceptions."

Malone nodded. "We got word of what happened to your… sister?"

"Sister," said Warsh.

Malone stretched out a hand. He was offering Warsh a business card.

"If you find yourself being questioned… Pressed. If you sense or feel you are in a situation where 'we' could be compromised… Call that attorney there."

Burn Everything... Then Forget It

SAN JUAN HILL

CHAPTER 19

There is no disgrace feeling absolute fear. He would feel it for years. The Express on the elevated would thunder through his being, crossing the years. It would never disappear because it would be a part of him, the part that would remind him death is waiting.

He had boarded the D train. He made his way to the front car. He would watch the city sweep past. He would study the station platforms where people waited like statuary for the locals. The city was now a masterpiece of cruelty and murder and he was one of its children portraits.

He looked back down through the car wondering—was he there somewhere?

He noticed the woman sitting in the seat closest to him. She had the same colored hair as his mother, the same slight build, the delicacy of movement.

She saw he was looking at her. She seemed to feel some tenderness toward him, maybe because he appeared lost.

"Are you alright?" she said.

He did not know how to answer.

She had a large cloth purse and held it toward him.

He did not understand.

She opened the purse, smiling lightly. She held it out.

He still did not understand.

"Look," she said.

He didn't know what he was looking for.

"In the bag. Look, in the bag."

He stepped toward her to be able to look in the purse.

The sunlight burned through the subway car windows. The train rocked. The wheels on the tracks made a scorching sound and what he was looking at there in the purse—a bloody knife.

CHAPTER 20

Charlie Dash heard the kid crying out two bedrooms away. Light from the hall fell across the bed when Charlie opened the door. A dark pathetic figure sat there crosslegged and shivering.

"Nightmare," he said to the boy.

"Nightmare," answered Billy.

Viola appeared in the doorway. "What's wrong?"

"Go back to bed," said her father.

"No."

Charlie got up and kicked the door shut. Then he went and held the boy's shoulders.

When the kid got settled, Charlie went downstairs. He kept to the dark.

This kid and what went down could unravel his and Warsh's life and this couldn't be.

You see, Charlie Dash lived on 247th Street and Independence in Riverdale. This was the upscale Bronx. It was part Scarsdale, part Rye.

Whites might be splitting from the Bronx for places like New Rochelle and White Plains but Riverdale was a different story. This was where well to do whites held firm at being well to do whites.

CHAPTER 21

After getting Billy home Charlie Dash took his daughter into Manhattan. There was something he wanted to show her.

He parked the Lincoln and stood with Viola looking into a dozen blocks of devastation that had been a run down tenement known as San Juan Hill. The blocks were hollowed craters where people had once lived and communed. It was a toxic battlefield of open lots, crumbled concrete, abandoned cars, endless trash and despair. And Viola could see children her own age playing there, wandering through the filth like marauders in an otherworldly blight.

"Why are we here?" said Viola.

He held his daughter's hand. He explained how this had been a neighborhood known as San Juan Hill. That most of the people living there had been black or Puerto Rican and those ruined streets were to be turned into a beautiful arts center and the poor who'd lived in those condemned buildings were promised affordable housing.

But that promise would never come to be. The residents there would be pawned off to the next slum or wretched ghetto. He did not tell his daughter this. Or that he had been part owner in one of the buildings. And he didn't confirm the racism behind this massive endeavor. An endeavor he was fully complicit in thought, word, and deed.

The murder of Billy's mother with its racist implications and the overthrow of the Guatemalan government said to Dash that the war between whites and people of color was going to expand mercilessly into every corner of life. That no one would be safe.

"I've been thinking," he said, "how good it might be for you to go away to school. Somewhere in Europe, maybe. You could get a great education. See other places. Meet other peoples. Think Paris."

This was a devastation to her. It said in the deepest reaches of her heart that she was unwanted.

"Don't you love me?" she said.

He knelt down and held her. "Of course I do. It's just that I see what happened to the boy and his mother and what is going on and I fear—"

"Are you ashamed of me… because I am not white?"

CHAPTER 22

There is no timeline for justice, and revenge may prove to be even more elusive as it not only demands the full complicity of your anger, but the laws of chance falling into your favor as well.

The boy would learn all this through tough experience. And a new Bill Castle would be shaped by the dark wisdom of the world.

Billy Castle went to a parochial Catholic school over on Hone Avenue where he was taught by nuns. When he returned to school he told everyone he wanted to be called Bill—and not Billy.

Standard operating procedure—the nuns only allowed students to go to the bathroom at the end of each period. So if you had to go—suffer. The one exception—if you were sick and went to see the nurse. Not long after his mother was buried, the girl in the desk ahead of him raised her hand and asked if she could go to the bathroom. That it was urgent. The nun looked at her watch, saw it was five minutes to end of class and that the girl could wait.

But she couldn't. Bill saw the girl's trembling legs, the feet moving, her wrestling with the weight. The nun was going on.

He'd seen moments like this before. But on this day in class, some force, maybe it was grief disguised as rage, had him standing up.

"Let her go to the fuckin' bathroom."

A death pall fell over the classroom. The nun set her classbook down. The students watched in mesmerized silence.

The nun took a strap from her desk drawer and started down the aisle. She pulled the girl up out of her seat. Saw that she had already urinated down her legs. The nun pushed her toward the bathroom door, then faced Bill.

"Bend over your desk," she said.

He was scared now, but he did not bend over the desk.

She ordered him again.

Again he did not obey.

She was slapping the end of the strap against one of her hands, and right in front of the boy's face.

She reached out with the strap. And whatever she intended to do, it didn't matter.

Bill ran right into her and knocked her back and over the girl's desk.

THE MARK OF SORROW

CHAPTER 23

So began the fall of Bill Castle, who was now the victim of an enemy known as sorrow. He was sent to an all boys Catholic school in New Rochelle, where he lasted less than a year. He was sent to another school—same result.

He abandoned school and roamed the city. He was arrested for stealing away overnight in a theatre on Fordham Road. He ripped off his uncle's booze. Bill absorbed the reprimands and punishments, the threats and the pleadings like a defiant prisoner of war.

He cut loose from all his friends and former schoolmates. Every day he passed under the Pelham Parkway station where his mother had died. He would go to Saint Raymond's Cemetery and it tore him apart that the grass at her gravesite was dried out and brittle.

His adolescence was... The Everly Brothers... The Shirelles... The Four Seasons... Ray Charles... Paul and Paula... The Ronettes... The Beach Boys... The Beatles... The Temptations... It was music he could attach memories to and piecemeal a life out of the unbearable unhappiness he had yet to escape, let alone defeat.

"You're going nowhere, man," said Warsh.

Warsh and the kid—now a tough, street smart, hard edged young man at the end of his teenage years—were in the downstairs apartment where Bill still lived. It was late, it was raining hard. The rain on the small metal awning over the front door was loud, brother, loud.

"Did you hear what I said?"

"I work at your gas station," said Bill. "I repair cars. I drive a truck and make deliveries for a furniture store. I pay my way."

Bill had never seen a psychologist or a counselor. He came out of a world where there had been no connection to any of that. You solved your problems or you died. Fait accompli. It was no different here. And as far as grief went, you got over it or you were gone. And when a person died, you took everything that was them, put it in boxes, and gave it all to Goodwill. He'd lived that as a boy when Warsh had brought in the neighbors' wives to help clean out the place but that was years ago. Of course, every time he heard the Express passing on the Esplanade he was captive to his past.

"You're going nowhere, man. You don't want to wind up—"

CHAPTER 24

He was having a moment with his uncle, but not in a mean hearted way. He went over and slapped the older man on the shoulder. "I get you, Papi. And I love you for it."

"My share of the gas station will be yours. And this house… yours. So you won't ever be wanting."

"I don't think I'm the long term gas station attendant type, Uncle. But thanks."

"Is there anything I can do?"

"Yeah," said Bill. "You can tell me what you're really about."

It was only the two men and the rain on a tin roof. Warsh said nothing. Bill watched him closely to see what he could pick up on his uncle's face.

Bill went over to the breakfront, got himself a cigarette. He walked, like nothing, over to the front door and opened it to the rain. He played the quiet out. His uncle played the quiet out.

"You're good," said Bill.

"That all depends on how you mean that."

"Nineteen fifty seven," said Bill. "Right here in this house. At night. A rainy night too. Charlie Dash showed up in his powder blue Lincoln. There were a couple of men with him in a second car. And both cars parked in the empty lot next door."

Warsh played the classic innocent pairing a shrug with an expression of uncertainty.

"There were any number of nights like that," said Warsh.

"Noooo. Not like this one. I was at the top of the stairs and Mom saw who it was and she shoved me off to my bedroom and told me to stay there. And when you went to answer the door she told you how she didn't want Charlie and those men in this house."

A car swept past, its headlights pouring across the open front door. A momentary glimpse of Bill's facial expression. A look of knowing.

"There were nights like that," said Warsh. "I can't remember one from the other, son."

CHAPTER 25

There was an unwritten book for that night that Warsh would carry with him to the grave. He thought of his sister, and well he should. At the front door that night Charlie had told Warsh, "Better bring a coat."

Warsh grabbed a slicker from a coat rack and the two men trotted down the walkway and into the lot next door where the cars were parked.

"Bad?" said Warsh.

"Bad."

"Is he—"

"Not yet."

"Where is he?"

"In the trunk."

They got into the second car parked beside the Lincoln. Miller was in the shotgun seat. There were men with him. One drove, the other in back. They were a young, well heeled war brigade. The types that are written about in the Daily News. Usually with a photo of their bodies lying dead on the floor of a barbershop or restaurant, and not doing work for the government. But you'd never know it looking at them. They could be Frankie Avalon or Fabian. As a matter of fact, that's what their people coined them.

As they headed down Matthews Avenue and onto Pelham Parkway in the rain, Fabian slapped the back seat. "Can you hear me in there, Nick?"

Nick could hear alright, because his own pleadings could be heard over the rain, the sloshing of tires, right through the leather seat and the trunk wall where Warsh was sitting. Warsh could almost feel the sobbing of the man coming right through the seat where his back was.

"Warsh... you up there? I know you're there."

"I'm here," said Warsh.

"I always did right by you when we were in Canada, didn't I?"

Warsh's mouth was dry. "Yeah... you always did right by me."

"I didn't scam money. I did not steal a delivery. You think I'd be that stupid to fuck with the government?"

"Yeah," said Avalon, calling out from behind the wheel. "I think you'd be that stupid. As a matter of fact we know you'd be that stupid. Because you're a degenerate gambler."

Charlie leaned around in the front seat and held out two nasty looking kitchen knives. He said to Warsh, "Take your choice."

What did it matter? Warsh took one without so much as a look.

CHAPTER 26

As they headed out the Hutchinson River Parkway, Fabian started slapping the leather seat where Nick was tucked away. He then began to sing "Bad Boy" by the Jive Bombers.

Avalon shouted, "We got to know who you scammed us with!"

"I didn't scam you. The load got taken."

"Then you should've died making sure it didn't get taken," said Avalon.

From the front seat, Charlie said, "Listen, boy. You can't save your life, but you can shorten the suffering."

Fabian was still singing away. It was madness.

They took the turnoff at Orchard Beach Road and they let Nick know they were on that road. It's heavily wooded all the way down Pelham Bay to Glovers Rock. On a good clear night there was hardly ever a car this late. A few drunken teenagers maybe. But with a heavy rain and a mist seeping in across the wetlands you could play out all kinds of psychopathic dramas without worrying about an audience. Nick knew that too and had descended into a state of uncontrollable panic, kicking wildly at the trunk wall.

It was madness and more madness. They drove on and they drove on and Fabian leaned over the seat from the back and pointed. "Right up there," he told Avalon. "You can see a post with a can tied to it. We marked it."

Avalon slowed as he got close and eased off the road, then turned down a dirt trail. Nick was deathly silent. *Madness,* Warsh thought, *sheer madness, and here I am with a box seat.* He looked down at the knife in his lap.

It got awfully quiet back there suddenly. The only sound the rain tapping away like pebbled teardrops along the roof.

"Maybe he had a heart attack," said Avalon.

Fabian stopped singing. He called to Nick. "Hey, honey... how's things back there?"

It was as if he were gone.

CHAPTER 27

"It's just up ahead," said Fabian, leaning over the seat.

He meant the grave. You could see it now in the rim of the headlights, where the soaked earth was piled up. Avalon shut the lights, crept along, then stopped the car and turned off the engine.

The men got out of the car with knives in hand. The ground was covered with dead leaves and branch rot and their shoes made this strange sucking sound as if the earth was working to take them down.

Avalon opened the trunk. Nick lay there, hands cuffed behind his back, beyond exhaustion now, beyond resignation. He even looked away from those grim shadows as if that meant the men with knives did not exist.

They stood around the trunk like some coterie of the depraved. Warsh looked to Charlie. The two men were standing on opposite sides of the trunk. Charlie was impassive, expressionless. What else could he be?

Fabian stabbed Nick with the knife. Nicking him just enough to get his full attention.

He gave up a couple of names in a defeated, emptying voice.

"You get those names down?" said Avalon.

Fabian repeated the names.

Avalon gave Fabian a tap on the shoulder. Fabian understood. He leaned over and drove the knife into the man's exposed back. He gave out a constricted cry. Then Avalon went at him. Charlie was next, and finally Warsh.

He prayed to God he would not freeze or falter in any way. And then he could not believe he prayed to God for such a thing. And with that he used the knife.

Avalon reached into the trunk for a burlap bag he had placed there. He collected the knives and put them in the bag and tossed the bag into the car.

Then they went about the business of pulling the body from the trunk, stripping it, getting it in the hole, covering it with the sodden earth, and topping it with dead leaves and branch rot. And when they left you'd think the earth had not been tampered with since the time of Adam.

CHAPTER 28

Warsh and Charlie were dropped off at the house on Matthews Avenue. The two men stood in the rain and talked before Charlie split.

"I'm going home to drink this night out of my system," said Charlie.

"The world's going mad," said Warsh.

"That's why people like me and you are here," said Charlie.

"I had no idea he was a screwhead."

"Traitor was more like it... He stole weapons earmarked for southeast Asia. Another bastion of communists and America haters where the weapons would have been put to use against us... Fuck him."

Warsh saw his sister peeking out of the dining room blinds.

"I don't like it... pretty boy taking all the knives."

"He probably wants to make sure they get deep sixed somewhere right."

"I hope that's it."

When Charlie drove off he honked and Warsh waved from the stoop like it was any old night. He hoped he could slip upstairs and avoid his sister. No chance. She was at the door with a towel that she tossed at him.

She looked over him grievously. He was soaked to the skin, hair streaked down his forehead.

"I don't want to talk about this," he said.

"I don't like that man."

"If it wasn't for that man I would not own half a gas station and the prime piece of territory it sits on."

"And this house... I know," said Mary. "I don't know what you're doing, but look at you."

"I'm wet from the rain," he said, drying himself off. Not looking at her, really. Which she picked up on.

"You're guilty, you know," she said.

"Guilty of what?"

"It doesn't matter... just that you're guilty."

"You have to be guilty of something. There's got to be more than just—"

She crossed her arms. She was clergy and judge all in one struck expression. "In case you haven't noticed," she said, "you have blood all down your trousers."

CHAPTER 29

Bill and his uncle were hard into the story of that night.

"I wasn't asleep," said Bill. "I heard you and Mom arguing… and one thing I remember is her telling you… you had blood all down your trousers."

Warsh was sitting on the couch, leaning forward, very much out of sorts. "I don't remember that," he said. "But whatever was said, it couldn't have been much."

"Funny that I remember it, but you don't," said Bill.

"We had lots of arguments. Mostly over nothing. We were brother and sister."

Bill studied his uncle. There was a lot going on in that man. "I figure you're lying to me… for my own good or your own good. But either way, you're lying to me, Papi."

A train came by on the Esplanade. The wheels kicking out great sparks in the rain. The track bridge above the street lit up in bursts. Warsh had this sudden rush back to the night he supposedly didn't remember. Who was it, Fabian, or was it Avalon who'd been singing in the back seat? Man, the two incidents so fleshed together sent a crawler up his back.

THE GIRL IN THE BABY BLUE LINCOLN

CHAPTER 30

Viola spent the better part of ten years going to schools in Europe. The only "parole" was the occasional holiday in the good old Bronx. She had a flair for romance languages but that didn't interest her as a career. It would prove to be her salvation in the underground life, without knowing yet, she was heading toward.

She'd come home unannounced and when she got out of the cab there was a handful of cars in the driveway and through the windows she saw what looked like a party of sorts. It was anything but.

She set her luggage down and rang the doorbell. She suffered a bout of uncertainty as she waited. Her father was not good with surprises.

Her father opened the door. She smiled. "Is this the Dash residence?" she said.

Talk about a shock. "Vy… what are you— Are you— Something wrong?"

"I left school."

He stepped back to get a full look.

"I've done my time," she said.

"I don't understand."

"I graduated early. You're stuck with me."

"Graduated? Early?"

"Yeah… They have their schedule, and I have mine."

"You mean you just walked?" said her father.

"It was a quicker pace than that. But essentially… yeah." She picked up her suitcase. "You gonna invite me in?" she said, walking right past her father. "The rest of my stuff is being shipped."

She saw about half a dozen people in the living room. The usual pedigrees her father ran with. Real civilization types. But a young girl out of nowhere appearing with a suitcase got their full attention.

"Hello, everybody… My name is Viola. You can call me Vy. I'm the prodigal daughter. Just escaped from the shores of Europe."

There was quiet detachment at first. Then it turned into polite hellos, introductions. She didn't recognize any of the people there.

A man in a well tailored three piece suit approached Viola. "My name is Mike Malone," he said. "I'm a longtime friend of your father's."

He was, to Viola, the classic WASPy American. And someone well suited to her father's attitude of mind.

"Question," said Mike Malone.

"Sure," said Viola.

"You part of the social revolution? End the war, voting rights, et cetera—"

"Card carrying member."

"Good for you," he said.

Of course he didn't mean it.

Viola glanced at her father. Saw the conflict and whispered into his ear, "At least look like you're glad to see me."

CHAPTER 31

By 1965 America was already in a deep state of internal conflict. One side called it necessary social change, the other a collapse into chaos. Both were true.

At that time the Vietnam antiwar protests were like fires across the county, lighting the flames against complacency, culminating in the 20,000 strong protestor army march on Washington. The number of protestors close to that of the troops fighting and dying in the jungles of 'Nam.

But that was only part of the human fissures cracking open the old state of things.

Civil rights... voting rights... women's rights... gay rights... protests over school segregation... housing... police brutality against minorities. The list grew and grew as the ugliness of America was in a death struggle with the promise of America that made it great.

CHAPTER 32

You could track the passion of the times by the spray painted pronouncements on subway billboards and tiled station walls. Street patriots with cans of acrylic on the march. Music lyrics appearing out of nowhere suddenly now became the proverbs of a new generation.

Bill was taking all this in, riding the subway up from Manhattan where he'd dropped off a delivery truck they'd done engine work on, when some antagonism started at the other end of the car.

There was a black kid who couldn't have been much older than Bill Castle. He was in an Army uniform. He was alone. He wasn't a big kid and there was a small pack of street toughs lording over his ass about being uniformed and in the Army and that he was a murderer and no "nigger" should be killing pathetic Vietnamese for the man.

They were antagonizing him pretty hard, dishing out all kinds of heated crap and ugly, ugly putdowns. The kid didn't want trouble and said so and he got his hat knocked off his head.

Bill caught a glimpse of himself in the subway window. He still had that raindrop scar on his cheek where the knife that killed his mother had a taken a little piece of him.

There were pages of a newspaper on the subway car floor and he bent down and grabbed a couple of them, and folded them neatly… then he reached under his T-shirt for a snub nose pistol he carried.

CHAPTER 33

Like nothing, he made his way up the subway car. There were a few people spread about, doing their best to be invisible. Bill walked right among the antagonizers and sat in the seat literally facing the soldier, who had no idea how to take this.

"You ain't your standard issue protestors, are you?" said Bill.

One of them in their number said, "You making a point here, boy?"

"Yeah," said Bill. "I'm about to give you a first rate introduction into going vigilante."

"What's that mean?"

He moved the newspaper from his lap and there was the gun.

CHAPTER 34

The kid in the uniform was named Rudy. He and Bill sat on a bench where the Grand Concourse and Fordham Road merged just down from Alexander's. The bench was outside the Army recruiting station for the Bronx. Rudy was there waiting on a ride to take him to his post in Jersey.

"You always carry a gun?"

"Mostly," said Bill.

Bill explained to Rudy how it came to pass. The train, his mother.

"Bad," said Rudy.

"You enlist?" said Bill.

"What...?! Drafted, brother. Maybe I get lucky and hook up with motor pool or electronics unit and am sent to Germany. You going to college?"

"I didn't even finish high school," said Bill.

"They're gonna draft your ass. Split to Canada."

Bill was looking at the recruiting station. "I could see myself enlisting."

"My cousin is over there. And you should see the shit he writes me."

Rudy's ride showed up. He and Bill swapped names and addresses. They shook hands. The recruiting station had his attention.

"Don't do anything stupid," Rudy said.

After he was gone, Bill sat back down on the bench and had himself a smoke. Then he went into the recruiting station and enlisted.

CHAPTER 35

Warsh was at home sitting in his recliner and watching the Yankee game when Bill came in. The Yankees were having their worst season in forty years.

"Get a beer," said Warsh. "And there's pizza. You can suffer this game with me."

Bill went over and shut the television off.

"I've got something to tell you, Papi."

"This feels like bad news," said Warsh.

Bill was standing in the doorway, leaning against the jamb. "I enlisted in the Army."

What Warsh felt at hearing this he couldn't share. All he said was "Why'd you do it?"

Bill took a long breath. He thought this out. "Why… because of what happened to my mother on the subway… Because I'm angry inside and always looking for a fight… Because I'm a fool and destructive and maybe I'll work that all out of my system. Because of all the lies around me… And how I'd like to be like you, before you became like you are… That way, if I don't die, we can face off against each other… And maybe I can get to love you and not feel guilty about it."

"That's a long 'Why' list."

"It could be longer."

"I don't understand all this," said Warsh. He did, of course, and was just lying for cover.

CHAPTER 36

Viola pulled into the Warsh gas station half a block up from the Pelham Parkway elevated. She was driving a used '63 Comet her father had gotten for her now that she was home. The attendant came out of the office wiping his hands on an oil stained rug.

"Would you fill it up?" Viola said. "Is Warsh around?"

"No...." The attendant pointed to the office. "But his nephew is."

"His nephew?"

There was Billy Castle... At the office desk, busy with paperwork... Damn... She hadn't seen him since he was eight... nine. She couldn't be sure. Everything she knew about him really was from that short time together in the blue Lincoln in the driveway soon after his mother's murder.

She wanted to get a better look and as he worked away she meandered over to his office. He was wearing a black T-shirt and black jeans. He was lean and his dark hair hung straight and it fell across his forehead. He was a mix of hard youth and adulthood. He finally looked up, sensing, she thought, that he was being stared at.

She nonchalantly headed for the office and went in.

"Can I help you?" said Bill.

Viola pointed to the cigarette machine.

She bought herself a pack of Marlboros. He'd gone back to a pile of invoices he was dealing with. She took to looking him and the scene over, without letting on who she was.

"Smoke Kool, huh?" she said.

He looked up. She was pointing to an open pack on his desk.

"Yeah," he said. "I like them sometimes."

She pulled her pack from the cigarette machine tray. She held them up. "Marlboro… *The Magnificent Seven.*" She hummed the melody as she tore off the wrapping and opened the box.

He took a moment there to check her out. Her skin was dark, and her black, black hair curly and wild and short.

There are some people who are more than the sum total of their features. Who are like that favorite record you remember that still hits you where you live. She was one of those, and it looked as though she didn't even know it.

CHAPTER 37

She flipped the conversation.

"You in college?" she said.

"College? I'm not even in high school."

Bill had a radio playing… The Byrds… "Mister Tambourine Man."

"I love that song." She knew the lyrics. Sang a chorus. "I don't sing worth a shit, do I?" she said. "No… don't answer that."

He just sat there a moment trying to catch up to her.

"I just graduated," she said.

"Where'd you go to school?"

"Europe," she said.

He sat back. "No kidding," he said. "Where?"

"Rome… Zurich… Marseilles."

"That must have been—"

"It wasn't," she said. There was no tone of kidding in her voice.

"You live over there, I guess."

"I'm… in transition."

"What are you doing here?"

"Getting gas, of course," she said.

"No··· I meant—"

She smiled. "I know what you meant."

"Ohhh," he said. "You're one of those."

"Yeah," she said. "But my heart's in the right place… Usually."

Out of the blue she came around his desk so she was close to him. "May I?" She reached for a pack of matches just inches from his hand.

"That's a nasty little scar you got there on your cheek," she said.

"Yeah," he said. This was definitely something he didn't want to talk about.

"Would you mind if I try something?"

"What do you mean?"

She took two of her fingers and kissed the tips and she went to touch the scar with them. His head pulled back but there was nowhere to go in the chair and she touched the scar with two soft fingers.

"What was that?" he said.

"You don't remember…." She took out a Marlboro and lit up. "Maybe you will one day."

By the time she reached the door it registered. He stood up. "The girl in the blue Lincoln… Charlie's daughter. Yeah, man. That was some dark time."

"I'll bet you don't even remember my name," she said.

"What do you want to bet?"

She grinned a long time before she answered.

"My virginity," she said.

TROUBLED SOUL

CHAPTER 38

Malone sat with Charlie in the den of his fine home in Riverdale. Charlie was being informed about his next task in service of the government.

In Vietnam they had taken to using herbicides to destroy the country. To defoliate the farmland and lush forests, to poison the earth and the people who lived upon it.

But there was another war going on. A second secret front even more clandestine in the bordering nation of Laos. There was an unnamed program of the most vile order with the toxic herbicide Agent Purple, even more destructive than Agent Orange, which they were using in Vietnam.

The details for delivery of the herbicide through private sources had been plotted out. But before Malone could finish up with the final details Viola returned to the house. They could hear her politely calling out, "I'm home," knowing her father was there with a guest.

She said "Hello" from the doorway. Called Malone "Mr. Malone." Noted he was in tie and jacket. The man was totally white bread. A phone call came in. It was Warsh.

"I have to take this," said Charlie.

Malone knew who it would be.

"Take your time," Malone said, standing. "This way Viola and I can get to know each other."

She got a couple of beers from the fridge and they sat on the patio.

"Your father tells me you're thinking about going to John Jay College of Criminal Justice."

"Thinking about it."

"And that you turned down admission to Harvard."

"Harvard is not my thing."

"What are you gonna major in?"

"Law and society."

CHAPTER 39

"Very heady stuff … and valuable. Your father ever tell you what I do?"

"No."

"I'm with a company called Democracy America."

"And what exactly does Democracy America do?"

"Ensures democracy, of course."

"And how do you do that?"

He smiled.

"By enlisting talented young people," he said, "with a passion for law and for society … For exactly what the College of Criminal Justice offers."

He leaned forward and spoke with easy and honest grace. "If you should decide on that college I can offer you specific internships that will count as credits toward your bachelor's degree. And even open up the possibility of paid sponsorship. Would you like to hear about it?"

She took a sip of beer, studying him all the while. He saw she was thoughtful and cautious. Both assets.

He took out a business card and handed it to her.

"Call me. We'll set a time to meet. But keep this just between us. I particularly don't want you mentioning it to your father."

She set her beer down. "Why not?"

"Because he might try and convince you it's a great opportunity for your future. It's always better if that comes from you first. That it's your passion. Then you can tell him."

CHAPTER 40

Viola was in the family room listening to the hi-fi when Malone's car pulled out of the driveway and her father entered the room. She was kicked back on the couch singing with the hi-fi, which her father could not stand. He shut off the damn thing to prove his point.

"So," he said.

"So," she shot back.

"What do you think of Malone?" he said.

"He always looks like a maître d' at a toney restaurant."

"I'm sure he'd love to know that. What did you two talk about?"

"Boring stranger talk… guess who I saw today?"

"I don't guess well."

"Billy… Bill… Warsh's nephew."

"Where?"

"At the gas station."

"What were you doing there?"

"Getting gas… He's a good looking guy… I think he's gonna ask me out."

This he didn't like at all but kept any expression of that under wraps.

"How do you know?" he said.

"I put my best spell on the boy."

"What the hell does that mean?"

CHAPTER 41

"It's a girl thing, Pop."

She got up and left the room and she was being followed the whole time.

"He's a troubled soul," said her father.

"Who?"

"You know damn well who I'm talking about."

"I hope not to shock you with what I'm about to say, but we're all troubled souls."

"Not like him."

She went right through the kitchen to the patio where she had left her cigarettes and a flat beer.

"Well... considering what he's been through...."

She took a Marlboro from its pack and lit it.

"What exactly does Mr. Malone do?" she said.

"He runs a 501 charity. A nonprofit. Raises money for setting up educational programs for children... third world country stuff. And when there's business opportunities that come along or government contracts for goods and services, he calls me in."

She blew smoke out her nostrils.

"Why you ask?"

"To get up to speed with the world around me."

"Don't discard what I'm telling you about that kid."

She looked at the burning tip of her cigarette. She was deep into her own thing. "Question," she said.

"Get on with it," her father answered.

"Is Bill trouble like Anthony Perkins in *Psycho* or like Steve McQueen in *The Great Escape*?"

"God damn you."

He walked up to Viola and took the cigarette right out of her mouth and he just crumpled it up in his hand and threw it away.

"What's really wrong?" she said.

"What do you mean?"

"You're still the old *you* I know so well."

"The *old* me knows of what he speaks."

"Is my coming home that much of a disruption?"

"I'd hoped you'd stay in Europe and got your college degree. Now especially with all this anti American chaos. Then maybe you'd come back home and go to Harvard."

"Harvard's a sitcom, Pop. And I couldn't have been handed a better time to come home. And what you call chaos… we call change."

"Well fuckin' excuse me," he said.

She was about ready to go off on him when her phone rang. Her father had set up a separate phone line for his daughter.

She went to the kitchen to answer it. Her father hounding along right behind her.

"Hello?" she said. "Hey! Hold on."

She covered the mouthpiece. "It's the troubled soul, Pop. Mind if I have some privacy?"

CHAPTER 42

He'd called her in spite of a run of nerves. He'd thought he should wait another day till he was more in the "I got this" groove, but he didn't.

He'd sloshed down a beer, it hadn't cut the edge. Nor did a couple of tokes on a joint. No courage there either. Youth sucks.

She'd caught on to his stumbling small talk and punchy silence. This was not a hit record in the making.

"You know what I'm thinking?" she said.

"No."

"It's a real drag having to call for that first date, isn't it?"

"I'm sweating it out."

"You did call to ask me out, right? I mean, I don't want to get too far out on a limb here."

"That's the plan," he said.

She noted her father in the hallway within earshot.

"By the way," she said, "my father says hello."

CHAPTER 43

There was a storage depot for pesticides off of Route 37 along the Raquette River, which was Mohawk Reservation country. Here trucks were loaded and stored with pesticides for crop dusters, spray trucks, and the like across the United States. Warsh arrived there with the paperwork to take a semi of the herbicide Agent Blue to Kentucky. Of course, the paperwork he was given back did not exactly conform with what was contained in the fifty five gallon drums.

There was a truckstop on Route 321 outside of Pigeon Forge, Kentucky, where he would park himself until his contact came along. The motel at the stop was one of those faux Americana jobs—you know—Daniel Boone frontier style log cabin with a plug in lightbulb fireplace.

In the middle of the night a call woke him. He would have a guest shortly.

He dressed and sat in the dark with only those twinkly lights of the cardboard fireplace. There was a painting on the wall above his bed he could not keep from staring at. It was of Daniel Boone, captured by the Indians, who were cutting his hair with long knives to the skin until all that was left was a scalp lock.

The scene had him flash on the murder he'd help commit out there by Orchard Beach. He'd always be captive to that little secret.

He'd heard footsteps outside. He got up and peeked out the blinds. Two men approached in the darkness. He saw one of them was Malone.

Warsh opened the door right as Malone knocked.

"This is a surprise," said Warsh. "What are you doing here? Something wrong?"

"Not wrong… changed."

Malone did not introduce the man with him.

"Give him the papers," said Malone.

The man had two passports and a folder which he handed to Warsh.

Warsh looked everything over. One passport was for him, the other for what was a Hmong priest.

"The truck is no longer your responsibility," said Malone. "Your job is to bring the priest to New York."

"Where is he?"

"Laos."

CHAPTER 44

Warsh knew what that meant. He was being sent to a military outpost deep in the Laotian jungle. It was an outpost that did not exist on any map, on any official document, that was nothing more than a rumor, not unlike the rumors the Conquistadores were told by indigenous Indians about mysterious cities of gold deep in the American desert. But this was not a city of gold, but an encampment of war.

This nonexistent outpost was in a valley high in the mountains that surrounded a runway on three sides. The nights could get cold there, the cliff faces would shroud in fog.

Warsh landed in a four seat Navion retread from the Korean War. He landed late in the day, in the shadow hours. There were CIA operatives, soldiers from Thailand, and Hmong rebels with their companies of children fighters.

This was the army that was going face to face with the communists. Another war, thought Warsh, another chance to change the face of the world, of course, another war brings death... and defeats. And all those kids cruising Fordham Road, going to movies and record stores and the Bronx Zoo would end up joining with those Hmong children on the same battlefield. His own nephew one of them.

The priest came out of a barracks hidden back in the trees flanked by a company of armed children and a CIA operative.

The priest was young, stocky, with a kindish face. He didn't dress like a priest either. Looking at him you'd think he was an Asian car salesman from Iowa. Which might not be too bad, when you get right down to it.

The shooting started once the priest got to the runway with his guard of Hmong youth. The automatic weapon fire came from the dark trees along the stripped down runway. One of the youth guards was brought to his knees, his back a huge bloody mess.

They hustled the priest into the plane as quick as they could. Thai soldiers and an American operative opened fire from the brush on the far side of the Navion.

An operative was talking with Warsh, shouting over the propellers. "The priest's English is minimal. French... yes. Vietnamese... yes. Our people will be waiting in New York."

A boy about ten standing alongside the priest was shot in the neck. He was lying in the shadow of the wing coughing up part of his throat. When the plane took off it went right over him.

Once the Navion had lifted off the runway and evaded the gunfire and ridden the sky until it cleared the mountains the priest looked at Warsh and made a fist and said in his chopped English... "America.... Freedom."

CHAPTER 45

The priest was being ushered to a safehouse in New York. He had been made "promises," been given "assurances of reward" if he would go through a series of debriefings. He would be felt out... tested. One minute you have a priest fighting the good cause against communists, the next minute he is secretly working for the Vietcong, the Russians, the Chinese. Was he a defector or a plant there to feed lies to a culture of vile colonialism?

BLEED

CHAPTER 46

Viola was in the downstairs hallway bathroom putting on the last touches of her makeup when her father walked past. He almost shit when he saw her there in her black fishnet body stocking and jean shorts with a telling hole in them on her butt and the tight T-shirt that had written across it—A WOMAN'S PLACE IS IN THE STRUGGLE.

"You look like something out of the Protestor's Guidebook," said her father.

She'd promised herself to not start anything so she just finished with her makeup and slipped on a beret.

"What do you know about struggle, by the way?" said her father. "You've gone to the best schools, you've been clothed, fed, housed, handed opportunity... So... what do you know about struggle?"

"I'll learn," she said.

She slinked past him. "Love you too."

Here came the sound of a growly motorcycle engine sweeping into the driveway. She made straight for the front door.

Bill hadn't even gotten off his Triumph when Viola escaped the house. Her father a couple of footsteps behind.

"Got a seat there for me?" said Viola.

Bill dusted the leather seat behind him with the back of his hand. She slung a leg over the rear tire and climbed on board.

To her father she said, "Say goodnight and have a great time."

Her father was giving Bill and that worked over Triumph a harsh stare.

"Hello, Mr. Dash," said Bill.

It was a stone wall Bill was staring into.

Bill booted that motorcycle into gear and sped out of the driveway.

"All of a sudden," said Bill, "I don't think your father likes me."

"You want my advice?"

"Sure."

"Don't think about it."

CHAPTER 47

It was a supreme night for cruising down the FDR on a Triumph making for Manhattan, skirting lanes, gunning it through traffic, gliding, tight as bodies can be leaning into the lanes they cut across. They didn't wear helmets back then so the wind did this wild rush through your hair and down the long of your face and the Jersey skyline across the river was beautiful and enticing in the balmy light of evening.

"You haven't even asked where we're going."

"That's just like me," said Viola.

"You haven't on purpose… Am I right?"

"All I can tell you is that I'm working on my ambience… How do you think I'm doing?"

When he outran a light and turned that Triumph onto 14th Street it became pretty obvious.

There were floodlights in front of the Academy of Music. And the concertgoers were mobbed all the way out into the street. On the marquee—

THE KINKS

It was their first tour of the States and they were already on the fast track to superstardom. They were the next chapter in the British Invasion that had landed on the shores of America to take the girls by storm.

They parked the Triumph over by Union Square and by the time they hustled it to the concert hall and through that crazed rabble flocked around the entrance they had jumped the wall of clumsy first date conversation and had each other arm in arm.

The concert hall was wall to wall rockers. The air dense, the sound ear splitting. The Kinks already had had a few hits in America... "You Really Got Me"... "All Day and All of the Night"... and when they played, in their primpy English outfits, with their wicked guitars, you felt the thrill of violence in their beat.

They were already known for fighting, fighting with others, fighting with each other. They were America in that way, only no one quite got it yet.

And when they played, when the band passed that turn in the road where rules are cast aside, it was pandemonium. Concerts, when they're on, really on, the passion is all consuming, and concerts become a grand poem of emotional hungers filled and personal mythologies created, that you will carry with you like some secret anthem.

Of course, what neither knew, not Bill, not Viola, was that halfway across the world their fathers had helped deliver contaminants to destroy a nation, to strip its jungle and its crop fields. To leave a nation destitute and futureless.

For them both, for Bill, for Viola, there was just that concert hall, that band, that experience, their fueled emotions for each other, while youth their own age in some faraway jungle were being condemned to the malefic poisons… That too would become part of their mythology. The mythology they created, and the one that created them.

CHAPTER 48

Walking out with the crowd into what was a perfect night Viola got behind Bill and swung her arms around his neck. "In Europe I heard about a bar," she said, "where singles go to meet and it's packed… Am I right?"

He nodded. "It's the thing now."

There were no singles bars back then. Not until a guy named Stillman who was hunting for chicks came up with what everyone thought a crazy idea. He'd buy a small bar, clean it up, give it the decor women like, the same with a menu of specialties, appetizers, and he would have a new breed of drinks concocted. Drinks that were sweet and appealed to the ladies.

It was on 63rd and 1st and it was called T.G.I. Friday's and it would change the landscape of America's drinking culture.

Friday's was so packed, from the front door to the bar, that you could die there and never hit the floor.

With a couple of Planter's Punch, Bill squeezed into what was little more than breathing space Viola had managed to stake out.

Bill handed her one of the glasses.

"Well," she said, "what exactly is this lovely looking cocktail with garnishes?"

"Planter's Punch… Dark rum, sugar cane juice, lime juice… I had them double up on the rum."

She tapped her glass against his. "Let's see what God had in mind when he created all this."

She took a sip... Then she took a reasoned swallow... then came a real swallow... Then her eyes lit up.

"A couple of these and you won't be able to tell the difference between a halo and a trash can lid," Bill said.

"This drink lies to you when it's going down," she said.

The crowd had them so pressed up against each other so Bill slid his arm around her, then slipped his hand into her jeans' back pocket.

"I hope that's you, darlin, otherwise I'm being robbed."

"You're being robbed alright," he said.

She threw her head back and laughed. She banged her head on his chest, then she gave him a passionate glance. He leaned down and kissed her. And what did she do? She laughed again.

"It feels like my face muscles are paralyzed," she said, "which means it's either you... or the drink."

CHAPTER 49

They were ripped when they left Friday's.

Outside there was a line of people around the block waiting to get in and unleash themselves. Viola began to sing along to a loud-speaker above the door tuned to WABC. The Sapphires doing their hit "Who Do You Love?"

Viola was even dancing, if you could call it that. Gyration was closer to the truth. The pathetic lost backup singer.

A mocking applause from the crowd. Whistles, even. She raised her drunken arms to acknowledge them, only to half stumble into the street. Luckily Bill caught her.

"I'm incredible," she said. "Aren't I?"

CHAPTER 50

They were walking up 1st Avenue where he'd parked the Triumph by Saint John's Church. They were in cocktail heaven and light on the chatter. And they didn't need those cartoon balloons over their heads with the usual first date packaged trivia of questions.

She yelled for him to stop right there in the middle of the block. He was caught miles off guard. "Question," she said.

She pointed at a darkened store front.

"Do you think you could trust those two?" she said.

It was their reflection in the shadowed window she was pointing at. Him with the collar up on his leather coat, and her with the beret set at a magazine cover angle.

He looked at their reflection a long time. They were like ghosts, waiting on the future. "I think you could trust them… it's the world you have to watch out for, anyway."

He started up the block.

"Don't forget to warn them," Bill added.

She followed behind him. Got out a cigarette and lit it.

"Man," she said. "You do deadly serious really well. I mean heartthrob well."

"I've had a lot of experience at it."

She caught up to him and slipped an arm over his shoulder as if commiserating with him. He took the lit cigarette from her mouth.

"You know what I think?" she said. "I think the world better get out of our way."

CHAPTER 51

They walked along and when they got to Saint John's, Viola took him by the hand and led him to the church steps where they crashed down and sat.

They were a drunken pair. Her with the cigarette now, one of her legs slung across his lap, blowing smoking rings nightward.

"Let's swap secrets," she said.

He looked at her like "What?"

"I'll share one with you... and you share one with me."

"Don't make my head strain," he said.

"I'll go first," she said. "I'm going to attend the College of Criminal Justice and this friend of my father he works with... Mr. Malone—"

"Michael Malone?"

"He's talking about offering me an internship for credit. But I'm not to tell my father anything until I meet with Mr. Malone and decide."

That was it, or so it seemed.

"That's not much of a secret," said Bill.

"That's not the secret... I think they're trying to co-op me... sucker me... that's the secret."

"Your father too?"

"The exigent circumstances of his life seem to have him by the throat... so it wouldn't surprise me," she said.

Bill stood up now.

"Your turn," she said.

He hesitated.

"I have a special fondness," she said, "for hesitation... not really."

The street seemed to disappear. Everything about it… disappear. He was alone inside his head. A stranger in enemy country. He couldn't even really look at her. He felt… he didn't know what he felt.

"I enlisted," he finally said.

"In the Army?"

"In the Army."

She was staring at him with something eons beyond numbing surprise.

"Did you tell Warsh?"

"I told Papi."

"He thought it was a big deal probably," said Viola. "Carry on with tradition and all that military crap. As they ship you off to Vietnam to die in an immoral war… with no hard feelings."

CHAPTER 52

He didn't want to hear this. And he told her so. He started off up 1st Avenue. She did not follow him. She shouted from the church steps.

"Where the fuck are you going?"

"I'm going to get the bike."

"It's not up there, it's down that way." She was pointing down 63rd. "It's just past the church."

He stopped. He wasn't sure. He was not only drunk, he was angry now, confused, and personally vulnerable.

"It's this way," he said, pointing up 1st Avenue. But he wasn't honestly sure.

"It's not that way… it's this way. And if you can't find your own motorcycle, then how well you gonna do in Vietnam?"

That was a slight that got him right where she'd aimed.

She was angry at herself for saying it but that fact only proceeded to further press her down the road. There was no stopping now.

He walked right past her and started down 63rd Street like she'd insisted where the Triumph was parked.

"Why would you do such an insane thing?" she said.

She followed after him.

"You could be throwing your life away."

Still no answer.

"Why would you do something that profoundly terrible to yourself?"

"I didn't know tonight would turn into a hate fest."

He was checking his pockets for where he'd stuffed his keys.

"This is not a hate fest!" she shouted. "It's the furthest fuckin' thing in the world from it. You hearing me?"

A couple of people passed them on the sidewalk. They had those "What the hell is this?" kind of stares that she picked up on.

"This is New York, man. Everyone screams on the street here, right?!"

He couldn't find his keys. She got hold of his arm. He was pissed he could not find the damn keys. He did not try to pull loose from her, though he could have easily enough. She held up one hand and there were the keys, jangling away.

"You gave them to me to hold," she said. "Very symbolic, don't you think?"

He grabbed them.

"Say something to me, something that resembles a reason for throwing your life away."

He literally repeated what he told his uncle. "I'm trying to put order back in my life."

She just stared at him. She had to orchestrate a thought around this statement of fact.

"That's not a reason," she said. "That's an excuse. Patriotism... good or bad that's a reason."

"It's not patriotism... It's about my mother on the subway... and the anger and frustration I live with... And I always have one eye open for a fight, as I have proven. I can be a fool and destructive. I thought, I go into the Army, maybe I could bleed out all the negativity from my system... short of my own death."

"That's the perfect word for it... bleed."

CHAPTER 53

The ride home was a masterpiece of uncomfortable silence. Yeah... she held onto him and, yeah... she rested her head from time to time against his back. He said a few perfunctory pieces of brilliance like "We got a sharp turn here" and "Hold on, I'm kicking it"... Not exactly unforgettable, not emotionally moving, not immortal icebreakers, certainly.

The Triumph pulled into the Dash driveway. It was past midnight and the beautiful homes with their huge lots and pockets of trees were all the more quiet, and the Triumph all the louder.

Viola caught a wisp of movement from the curtains in the darkened breakfast room... the eye of Judgment.

She slid her leg up and off the motorcycle. Then there they were in the disquiet of the night having to make some kind of goodnight, goodbye, good riddance, good something or other.

She bit her lip and took that jump into the intimate gray of uncertainty.

"I didn't mean to hurt you," she said. "And for that I'm—"

He put a hand up to stop her. "Best intentions," he said. "I get it."

"Do you?"

"I have to deal with those intentions a lot myself, and I often come up quite short."

"We've had our first fight," she said. "And we haven't even got laid yet."

He put the Triumph in gear. She told him to hold it a moment. She went over and kissed two fingers and then touched the raindrop scar on his cheek. Just as she had that day at the gas station and that very first day in the blue Lincoln in the driveway of his house after his mother's murder.

Oh my God, she thought—

The house was conspicuously dark when Viola walked in. She called out, "I know you're lurking back there."

Her father came up the hall from the breakfast room.

"Like I'm an eleven year old," she said. "You waiting up to check me out... Aren't you gonna ask me how my date went?"

"Badly, I hope," he said.

"The god of judgment has spoken." She started upstairs. "Th-Th-Th-That's All, Folks!"

CHAPTER 54

She was alone in bed smoking a cigarette and looking up at the piecemeal shadows of herself on the ceiling. Mysterious Viola Dash meet distraught Viola Dash. She was alone there with a heaven of conflict and unsettled emotions. She had questions bearing down on her by the name of Billy Castle.

He was not the youth, the man, she had thought he was. He was something else, something more. And that's what suffering and sorrow can do for you. They expand the world of your life and create sometimes someone who will struggle for standing.

He was a person who had looked at himself honestly and could tell you, without trying to save face, the facts of himself. Who could admit to being foolish and destructive and knowing it, be at war with it, and would give himself up to it, to overcome it.

A few questions about herself came calling. Why had she become so angry at the church? Why was she so angry at herself for becoming angry at the church?

And why was she so… frightened? Yeah… frightened. Using that word was honest to a fault.

Did he know the entirety of existence better than she? The taking of one's mother so violently leaves an indelible curse upon your consciousness, for sure. A reality she knew well of through her adopted mother's own battle that laid waste to the flesh.

It was even more than that. She was connected to him in ways she could not explain, ways that were not yet even written. And it was not the dreamy desires of youth. It was not some sentimental fantasy walking hand in hand with lovesick devotion. She knew just this much. He had a place in her life that she would not meekly surrender.

CHAPTER 55

"I need your advice," said Charlie.

"Advice," said Warsh. He stopped pouring coffee.

He set the pot down. "Count your blessings, and leave no forwarding address."

"Under different circumstances I would think that funny."

"It wasn't meant to be funny. Now... shall I get back to pouring you coffee or should I stand here urgently still?"

They were in Warsh's kitchen. He went back to pouring both of them a cup, and then he set the pot back on the stove.

"Bill and Viola.... You know they went out with each other."

"I didn't, as a matter of fact."

"If they should become a thing. And start comparing little emotional notes from their pasts, who knows where they will—"

"I hear you."

Warsh took up his coffee, then he set it back down. This was a reality that wears thin.

"He's trouble," said Charlie. "Let's be honest. The boy is violent, destructive—"

"You're making your point. Heavy handed as it is."

"I don't want my daughter around him," said Charlie. "And I think you wouldn't either."

"It might be us," said Warsh, "they shouldn't be around."

Charlie took a deep and frustrated breath.

"You can never be too careful about being too careful," said Warsh.

"Amen," said Charlie.

"I don't think we have to worry here."

"No?"

"Bill enlisted yesterday."

"What? Army? Navy?"

"Army."

"We can talk to Malone. He might be able to have him shipped to Vietnam."

Warsh looked like Charlie had put the Kiss of Death on him.

"That's my boy you're fuckin' talking about."

"You're right. I wasn't thinking. You handle it with Malone any way you see fit."

"Fate's gonna handle it… not me."

CHAPTER 56

A door down the hall opened and out stepped, of all people, the priest taken from Laos.

"What the hell," said Charlie, "is he doing here?"

"There was an issue at Bedford Street. Malone is on his way here. He'll take over."

The priest was standing in the kitchen doorway. He was wearing a Yankee sweatshirt, grimy loose trousers, and sandals.

"He looks like some Bronx back alley junkie," said Charlie.

The priest was speaking French, which neither of the men understood. He was pointing at the coffee pot.

Warsh went into the kitchen and got out a cup, sugar, milk. Waved a hand over it all, motioning for the priest to drink.

"He better be all that he professes," said Charlie.

The two men were looking the priest over. He had no idea he was being handled. He was sipping at his coffee, smiling here and there.

"Imagine if he knew what we were saying," said Charlie.

"Imagine if he knew what we were thinking," said Warsh.

"Yeah," said Charlie. "Wait till they get a couple of doses of LSD in him."

CHAPTER 57

Bill was pushing that Triumph of his up the Grand Concourse, slicing his way through the traffic, cutting it all a little too closely, cursing under his breath, tossing in a lot of that "Who do they think they are?"

He had an envelope between his teeth, the edges of it flapping away with the wind. He was just coming back from a meet at the Army enlistment headquarters on the Concourse just down from Alexander's.

He had sat before the officers in charge there in absolute silence. The perfect soldier confronting the insurmountable dilemma.

The day was hot, the air grimy. It was perfect Grim Reaper weather.

He ran a light, he ran another, he taunted a city bus, passed an oncoming police car doing way over the speed limit. He nodded to our city's finest in a flashing goodbye.

His shadow there under the elevated, the sun coming through the gray oxidized girders, moving so fast the image was like something part man, part machine.

CHAPTER 58

Bill was just pulling into the driveway when Warsh and that small entourage was leaving. He'd seen Malone a few times over the years, but Malone offered the kid hardly even a hello. This day was no different. When that crew was together they acted like the chosen ones, even his uncle, which turned off Bill. The Asian wearing Warsh's Yankee sweatshirt was completely baffling.

"Hey, boy," said Charlie, walking past Bill. "I hear you enlisted. Good for you. You're on your way to becoming a full throated American."

As he got older Bill liked Charlie Dash less and less. He could feel the bad vibe in his tone. Maybe that was it.

Warsh and Bill talked alone for a moment. "What's with the Oriental dude?" said Bill.

"We'll talk later… Everything alright?"

"No," said Bill.

CHAPTER 59

"What can you tell me about Mary Buergos?" said Viola.

Her father looked up from the desk in his home office where he'd been trading phone calls.

"Where the hell did that question come from?"

"From your one and only precious daughter, that's where."

She entered the office. She copped a cigarette from the pack on his desk.

"So… what can you tell me? Was Bill tight with her? Was she a good mother? Were there things about her that moved you? How come Bill's last name is Castle and not Buergos or Warsh?"

"What do you want to know for?"

She struck a match. She lit the cigarette. She inhaled. She blew out the smoke slowly. She crossed her arms. She waited.

"Well?" he said.

"Because I want to know… *him*."

"Why not just ask *him*… yourself?"

"Because I'm asking my father."

He sat back.

"As you get older I begin to see that you would make someone a serious adversary."

"Thanks for the compliment."

Her father placed his hands firmly on the back of his neck like he was trying to soothe away some pain. He hated little detours like this that touched upon his own life in any way. Even for his own daughter.

"Bill's name was changed to keep the newspapers and reporters away so the boy could have a life. So he wasn't exploited. They're all exploited. The victims. All of us, I guess. Warsh even moved a couple of times.

"Gardner Flynn handled everything. He's an attorney who lives over on Bronxwood and Mace, as I recall. You probably don't remember him. He was a paperwork genius. Birth certificates... Social security... Adoptions. You name it."

"Did he handle my paperwork?"

Her father just stared at her. "You got too many questions for my taste."

"I'm just curious."

"Bullshit. Flynn is also a mafia attorney. And a fag."

"So what does that mean?"

"It means he's connected in deep, dark ways. To deep, dark players."

CHAPTER 60

"There was much goodness in that woman," said Charlie. Goodness as a kind of holiness. She didn't have much of an education. She worked in a candy store on Webster Avenue. It's still there.

"When your mother was sick Mary quit her day job and got a nightshift job working as a janitor. This way she could be with your mom here till I got back from work."

Charlie Dash looked to be caught up in that memory of the old days.

"She took care of you too when I wasn't around. You're too young to remember. I don't know if Bill is the way he is because of the murder. I do know that he came out of the womb ready to rumble. A lot could also have to do with his father."

"I thought he was never—"

"He was around a few times."

Charlie's mood blackened.

"He'd take Mary's money, then he'd beat the hell out of her. The night she died I couldn't get back here soon enough. Mary was lying in bed beside your mother while she took her last breath. And Mary stayed there till I got here."

He saw his daughter had been moved, and thought it best to stop right there. He had been honest in what he told her, except he'd left out much… such as the truth.

CHAPTER 61

When Warsh returned home the front door to Bill's apartment was open. Bill was nowhere to be found, but the landscape of the kitchen told the story... four empty beer cans on the table... a dirty full stubbed ashtray... the cap to a scotch bottle nowhere to be found. The door to the basement was open. The light in the basement was on. And from the basement came a sound Warsh knew all too well—a quick and then a sharp thud.

"I'm coming down," said Warsh.

Another whoosh, and then that sharp thud.

The basement was an unofficial family room. Couch, chairs, television, little used Ping-Pong table now covered with junk and some old Lionel trains. One basement wall had been faced with cork and used for target practice.

Bill stood beside a table with an assortment of stilettos, switchblades, and nasty killing knives. He was taking them, one by one, and then throwing them at a target on the wall. Taking a moment here and there for the obligatory drink of scotch.

Warsh noted that the target pinned to the cork wall was an official looking letter of some kind.

"You want to tell me what this is all about?"

"Remember when you set all this up?"

Warsh remembered, of course. He had taken the boy back in 1960 to see The Magnificent Seven at the Loew's on Fordham Road. And there was James Coburn, a cowboy gunfighter, who did not use a pistol to outdraw his enemies, but only a knife.

It was after his mother's murder and Warsh thought this might be good for him. Something to burn off all kinds of bad energy.

"You want to tell me what the letter says?" said Warsh. "Or do I chance it?" He pointed to the wall.

"Chance it," said Bill.

Bill sat in the chair beside the table and lit a cigarette while his uncle removed the knives that had found their mark.

He read the letter. It was on military stationery. Bill Castle had been formally rejected by the Army. In very cut and dried language it said a heart murmur had been discovered during his routine entry examination. The long term diagnosis was unclear and demanded further investigation.

"You know what a heart murmur sounds like?" said Bill.

"I barely know what one is," said Warsh.

Bill took up a knife, a time worn dagger from his uncle's collection. And sitting there at the table he flung it at the cork wall.

There was that whooshing sound and then a sharp thud.

"It sounds like that," said Bill.

THE MAN WITH THE GOLDEN GUN

CHAPTER 62

Warsh sat down. Bill and his uncle remained there in that funky basement. Warsh reached for the scotch bottle. Bill slid his glass toward the older man. Warsh poured a heady glassful. The ground level windows were like grimy eyes staring down at them.

Bill looked around… the Ping-Pong table… the Lionel trains… baseball glove… bat… a bureau where some of his mother's old clothes were stored away… a fake gold Christmas tree.

Bill waved an arm. "The family basement… where all memories come to die."

"You can't see it like that," said Warsh.

"Even if it is?"

"Especially if it is."

For a moment Bill glanced at the phone. Warsh caught the look, the conflicted expression.

"You shouldn't see her."

"You're probably right."

"It's not about me… It's about her father."

"Translated… the great disrupter is fucking up orderly lies… including yours."

"Some things are not meant to be controlled… I read that somewhere," said Warsh.

"And you've been sitting on it for just the right moment."

Bill got up. He took the scotch bottle. He didn't need a glass. He paced about the basement looking over old memories. He raised the bottle. “Like the rebellious youth that I am.”

He took a drink. He went over to the gold fake Christmas tree leaning against the wall. He ran his hand over the tinseled branches. “I don’t know what Mom saw in this fucking thing.”

“She liked it when the lights were on.”

It still had rows of white Christmas lights. Bill knelt down. Looked for the plug and then stuck it in an outlet.

A dozen of the lights strung on the tree flicked on, then they flicked off, and after a few seconds flicked on again, and in a ghostly fashion slowly began twinkling.

“After all these years,” said Warsh.

The basement was turned into some mysterious place of aura and shadow and gripping quiet.

“Surreal,” said Bill.

“I’d like to think that’s my baby sister there,” said Warsh. “And that she’s talking to us.”

Warsh ran a palm across his eyes and Bill noted he was crying. He walked over to his uncle and took hold of his shoulder.

CHAPTER 63

She was sitting on the stone patio behind the house, a patio covered with trees that had been there for decades. Trees she had climbed as a child, a few board remains of a treehouse built by her father for her. Her name barely visible in the rotting paint.

She sat at a stone table, her chin resting on an upturned fist. Her father stood at the open French doors. “What are you doing?”

“I’m pretending I’m Isaac Newton,” she said.

It took a moment for her father to remember who Newton was. "How's it working out?"

"My glowing mind is not delivering."

He walked out to the patio.

"What are you trying to solve?"

"I'm trying to figure out what might help Bill to—"

"Give him a year killing gooks in the jungle... That ought to give him some perspective on life."

He saw that didn't go over well with his daughter. That he was being an asshole.

"I'll remember all this, Pop... when I write your biography."

He turned away. "You want to help him?"

"Yeah."

"Bring his mother back. And if that doesn't work... forget him."

CHAPTER 64

Bill was out front having a smoke. Trying to catch up in his mind everything that had been happening. Warsh joined his nephew.

"Anything else you thought you might like to pursue?" said Warsh.

"Sure," said Bill. "I got a whole list of adventures I have lined up, it's just—" He felt around in his shirt pocket, in his pants pockets. "I seem to have misplaced them."

"Boy, you cast a hard shadow sometimes."

"Me... I'm just a cuddly rattlesnake."

Warsh threw his head back and laughed.

"I know what all this is about," Bill said. "You and Charlie don't want anything that will disturb this little ring of military contractors you got."

"Our work is charted for the security and integrity of this country. And Dash is worried his daughter is vulnerable and she doesn't need to be around—"

"You were about to say something you'd regret. Right, Papi?"

Warsh nodded.

"When we have these conversations I feel like we're dots on the earth," said Bill. "And in case you and Charlie hadn't noticed, Viola Dash is smart. She's gonna get on to you and her father whether I'm in the picture or not."

"I will repeat what I said before," said Warsh.

"Security and integrity," said Bill, "but with a little well paid pain and drama from time to time. Mom said things along the way, by the way. And they don't quite confirm your description of events."

"Fuck you," said Warsh.

Not long after that Bill's phone rang and he came to answer it. Warsh followed, but stopped in the hallway.

"Something will come along," said Bill, parroting his uncle. He pointed at the phone. "Maybe this is it."

He went to answer it, but then he didn't. He stared at the phone, then at his uncle.

"You try to take bold measures in your life and what happens?"

The phone kept ringing. "Fate quietly intervenes."

Bill took a cigarette from a pack in his shirt pocket and walked out, leaving the phone to keep ringing.

CHAPTER 65

Viola had gone to the College of Criminal Justice campus to pick up some admissions paperwork. There was a rally going on—YOUNG PUERTO RICANS FOR JUSTICE. One of their number spoke to the crowd through a bullhorn.

The Civil Rights Act had been passed the previous year. A landmark that meant to end discriminatory practices in housing, employment, segregation in schools, in federal programs.

The act gave the oppressed a foothold in the promise of America. Practical application, of course, was another and darker story.

The rally was about building an army of the determined—black, Puerto Rican, Caribbean, and white—to enforce the 15th Amendment through the Voting Rights Act.

"I'm American," said Viola, when asked by a rallier.

"That sounds like an evasion," said another of the activists.

They all started making comments among themselves about Viola's answer. Some biting, most politically grounded. One statement, decidedly pointed, was "You mean American white or American Puerto Rican? Or are you nothing at all?"

CHAPTER 66

Bill swung his Triumph into the family gas station on Pelham Parkway. He noticed there was someone in the office, their black cowboy boots up on the desk, the seat back, whoever he was, was holding up a *Playboy* magazine, checking out the open centerfold.

"You look very comfortable," said Bill as he walked into the office. "Can I help you?"

"Maybe."

There was a funny gruffness to the man's voice. He swung his feet off the desk, he sat forward, he lowered the magazine.

Bill saw then that the man behind the desk with the Playboy was not a man at all.

Viola held out the magazine, flashing the nude centerfold. "Ursula Andress is some piece of ass. Isn't that how you guys like to describe chicks… She's some piece of ass?"

"You jujitsued me."

"Yeah… I was playing with you a little bit. This issue… has the third installment of Ian Fleming's The Man with the Golden Gun. She put the magazine down. "It's not Goldfinger, but it's pretty good."

Viola tried to copy Shirley Bassey and sing a few lines of the Goldfinger theme song.

"I sound like—"

"Even worse," said Bill.

Viola got up. She stretched. She was wearing black jeans and a tight sleeveless T-shirt and with the light through the office windows on her she left a lingering image.

"I called you earlier," she said. "But you know that, don't you?"

"Yeah… I just wasn't into answering the phone."

"You knew it was me?"

"I knew."

She'd walked to the street. The Pelham Parkway elevated station, in all its dismal concrete gray, was within shouting distance.

"You and your mother were on the train that had stopped right there, at that station, when it happened?"

"Yeah," he said. "And maybe someday I won't remember it like I do."

"You ever chase the answer as to what happened?"

"No," Bill said.

He started for the gas station garage.

"Where you going?" said Viola.

"I got a date with a transmission."

"Are we getting together tonight?"

"No," said Bill.

"Good... I'll pick you up at your place," said Viola. "Around eight."

CHAPTER 67

Bill had lied. And he didn't like it. He was just not ready.

The summer of his mother's death he took to the elevated station at Pelham Parkway. And there he began asking questions of the people who got on and off the trains.

Holding up an artist's sketch of the suspect who had stabbed his mother to death—*Do you know this man?—Excuse me, have you ever seen this man?—Pardon me, ma'am, I need help—*

Day after day in a hoarse, broken voice, his own wounds not completely healed, he walked the concrete platform so long he imagined that he left scars in the concrete from endless hours of footsteps.

He never told his uncle, who only found out when a reporter rang his doorbell after having heard about "the boy at the Pelham Parkway station."

Warsh took the boy home and ordered him to quit this madness. It did little good. Bill returned, was taken home, returned again, and yet again. The endless war of agonizing emotions. Warsh felt guilty he was even in this tug of war for the boy's heart.

When school started his uncle received a call from the nuns that Bill had not been in class for a week. Of course, he was easy enough to find. It was a woebegone reality that played out in the heat, in the rain, in the snow, in the grimy slushy waste along the sidewalks, until he was expelled.

There was no more punishment, no more school. He spent his days with Warsh at the gas station learning how to repair cars.

He was carrying the weight of death upon his shoulders and finally out of pure exhaustion he gave up. He blankly helped his uncle set up the gold Christmas tree that his mother had so loved. And every night, he slept beneath that tree with its twinkling lights, hoping God would take mercy and grant him one great prayer.

CHAPTER 68

She found out a few hours later Bill had lied to her. And how did this happen?

Viola had driven over to the Bronx Historical Society on Bainbridge Avenue. She began a search. She knew the date of the murder—June 19, 1957—and she had a list of all the local newspapers that existed at the time. The major newspapers of the day were out of the picture. None had covered it. After going through all the local papers' dead files she found one article, two paragraphs long, in the *Bronx Press Review*.

Five days later, in that same weekly, with no suspect in sight, an artist's sketch had been rendered from the half dozen or so people on the train and the station platform who had given their description of the assailant. The sketch had been published in a follow up article—which was also a final article.

The face did not strike fear in the hearts of man, or woman. The assailant was a plain looking fellow, maybe twenty five, with a crew cut and those thick, black rimmed Superman glasses.

The only detail, really, about him was the article's reference to "racial epithets" he'd been screaming as he slashed Mary Buergos to death.

CHAPTER 69

Viola sat in a hipped up coffee shop on 205th Street. It had a real Caribbean feel to it. Caribbeans were part of the new Bronx migration. It was mostly a young crowd. A real Dobie Gray "I'm in with the In-Crowd" kind of feel. The walls were flush with posters, total homegrown art about the Voting Rights Act that was being fought over in Congress and on the streets.

Viola sat alone with a notepad and pen. She was going over the newspaper clipping of the murder, and the artist's rendering of the suspect. Talk about faded history, and how it was part of the moment at that very time.

She wrote down—The unanswered question—Why had the suspect been ranting about Mary Buergos being a Puerto Rican? She didn't pass for African or Spanish. She was your typical Caucasian housewife. Bill was part Puerto Rican but you'd hardly know it when you'd look at him at eight.

She took a few moments thinking on this, and as she began to draft a personal ad she intended to place in a few of the local newspapers, the very nature of race itself overtook her thoughts.

The students on campus who had called her out, wanting to know if she was Puerto Rican or not. Her answer—I'm an American—seemed not good enough, not sincere enough, not right enough, not enough, period.

She considered this in relation to his own family. Her father had racial animosities. She'd heard him insult blacks, Italians, Jews. She did not believe her father was ashamed of her for being Puerto Rican, but maybe she was a subtle black mark on his life. And that could have been one of the reasons he sent her off to Europe all those years ago.

CHAPTER 70

One day that always came to mind was when she and her father were coming back from the Warsh house on Matthews Avenue not long after the murder, where she met Bill for the first time.

Coming home her father sidetracked into Manhattan to the San Juan Hill neighborhood, which was a crumbling shell of blocks that was to become the illustrious Lincoln Center. A few blocks whose history summated the world. How these poor slum blocks had been handed over to the wealthy to be turned into an architectural masterpiece for its entertainment.

The poor were moved along like cattle. And it wasn't just about a class divide. It was about altering the world. Where one side demanded its right, its superiority, which was white, by its very nature. The poor immigrant did not even have a say in their own destruction. And rules. All rules meant power. Power that was dominating, was its trademark. And that power was white.

The poor of San Juan that day were to disappear, forgotten into worse and poorer neighborhoods of neglect—only to be born again and to reemerge like some empirical phoenix in little coffee shops and places of business like where Viola was sitting with the sun of 205th Street beating down on the window beside her.

That day with her father. Showing her the San Juan neighborhood and explaining the world to her had made her uncomfortable in a way she could not understand.

But it was the same feeling she had when the students on campus confronted her, and it was a discomfort she reluctantly felt in her father's presence of late.

Not that he did not love her. She felt he did. But there was something off, something ill placed, ill defined, illy lurking in their unspoken relationship.

She put all that out of her mind and went back to drafting the personal ad. The waitress came over with a check and a flier... this flier listed all the rallies and protocols for the upcoming Voting Rights Act. Viola paid at the counter on the way out.

There was a copy of a photograph taped to the back of the cash register, she noted. It was hundreds of protestors in front of a brick wall. And on the wall, in flashy acrylic paint, it read—AMERICA WILL NEVER BE THE SAME AGAIN.

CHAPTER 71

Gardner Flynn was a noted attorney. He had been instrumental in the adoption paperwork of Viola Dash. Supremely educated and television starish, forty. Impeccably dressed, impeccably mannered. He was also quietly gay, and the attorney most important and influential people sought out who had been compromised by their sexuality.

He lived on the corner of Bronxwood and Mace, in a three story brick house that was classic old world Bronx.

The house was across the street from Saint Lucy's Grotto. The Grotto—if you don't know the Bronx —was a copy of the Lourdes Shrine. It had a huge manmade cave and statue of the sainted lady where water poured forth around her bare feet. And there were benches facing the cave where people in all states of desperation and need came to be one in prayer with the revered woman.

Beside the front door was a plaque that read—LAW OFFICES OF GARDNER FLYNN—and a buzzer, which Viola rang.

A moment later a voice responded on a small speaker. "May I help you?"

"My name is Viola Dash. I would like to discuss Mr. Flynn representing me in a matter."

A very long silence followed that before the front door opened. What looked to be a woman of sixty or so answered. She wore a man's suit, she had a man's haircut. She invited Viola in.

The house was elegantly and expensively decorated. Mid century, top of the line. Viola was asked to wait in the living room, which was virtually a law library. Music played softly from somewhere. Very uptown stuff.

The woman had gone into a back office. Through a slightly open door Viola saw her talking with someone who probably was Gardner Flynn. When the woman returned she pointed to the door.

"Mr. Flynn will see you."

"Thank you," said Viola.

It had all gone down with such quiet and class.

CHAPTER 72

As Viola entered the office, Gardner stood. She glanced around the room. It was like everything else—elegant and expensive.

"I look out of place here," said Viola. "Don't I?"

"You'd be surprised," said Gardner, "what out of place means in this place."

He'd already come around the table and hugged her. "The last time I saw you," he said, "you weren't wearing fishnet stockings and cowboy boots. But you were as good looking."

As he embraced her, she saw on a breakfront beside them a photograph of Gardner and Viola's mother in their school uniforms out front of Saint Lucy's School.

She lifted the framed photograph and pressed it to her heart.

He nodded. Then he had her sit.

"Now," he said, sliding in behind his desk. "What could you possibly need the services of an attorney for?"

She carried a legal pad and folder and she passed him the folder. At first he feared it might have something to do with her adoption or birth parents, which was a world he did not ever want to touch, as it would demand lying.

What he first saw was a copy of the June 1957 article in the *Bronx Press* about the murder of Mary Buergos. And the second article with the artist's sketch of the suspect.

It was a story Gardner knew all too well. He also saw Viola had written out a personal ad:

5,000 dollar reward
for information leading to suspect
in the murder of Mary Buergos
On the IRT Dyre Ave Line
June 19, 1957
Contact:

CHAPTER 73

"I have the five thousand dollars. I didn't go to my father for the money. That's from the insurance trust my mother left me. Which you know about, of course. I can write you a check, including paying you for your time."

He waved for her to settle down.

"Does your father know about this?"

"No."

"Does Warsh know about this?"

"No."

"Does Bill Castle know about this?"

"No… but he will."

"Why are you doing this?"

"I'm trying to save a life."

"Save a life… Bill?"

"Change a life, I should say."

"You don't actually think this will take you to some conclusion?"

"I thought it might be better if I had your law offices as the contact. You could take the information and pass it to me."

"You slipped past my question, young lady."

"I'm trying to find something to give him… faith… direction… a reason…."

"You know what kind of people will contact you when they see the reward? You'll have every denizen from the deep coming out of the woodwork. Some might be dangerous."

"If it's something you'd rather not take on... I would understand."

He waved for her to stop.

"If you end up going forward... I will take care of it."

"If?"

"I'm talking to you as your attorney now. I want you to take a day... no... two. Weigh out everything. Then if you're still *mad* enough to go forward. If you think this could actually achieve something that would help Castle in some way... Go for it."

THE WHITE HORSE

CHAPTER 74

After Viola had left, Gardner took the photograph which had been left on the desk and went out into the hallway. He looked like a man who had gotten bad news.

His paralegal noticed the change in him. "Are you alright, Mr. Flynn?"

Without answering, he suggested she shut off the lights and go home. Before she had even left the house, Gardner was on his way to getting very drunk.

Once alone with a glass peaked in bourbon he went and sat on the stairs up to the second floor. He looked over the scene of the crime, the scene of the humiliation, and the desperate stupidity that never really goes away, that is not a menacing blur, but rather a choking succession of real lived moments. Even the great lawyer in him had been deceived into believing the past could be outsmarted.

It had rained that night years ago. A rain that left him anxious because Viola's mother was supposed to call, but she hadn't called, and he'd promised not to call.

Then headlights flared across the driveway and over Gardner's house on Bronxwood. The frantic door buzzer followed, a fist slamming against the heavy wooden door. It was Viola's mother calling out to him from the porch.

She stood in the open doorway. She was crying, but that was not near the worst of it. Her mouth was bloody, her nose was bloody. One of her sharp cheekbones was heavily discolored. She was soaked to the skin. She was missing a shoe.

He helped her into the house. He closed the door and locked it and put the chain on it.

"He found out," she said.

Gardner helped her to the office. He tried to steady her down with a drink. He went to the hallway closet and came back with a bath towel.

"Dry yourself."

She was shivering so.

"He'll be coming here," she said.

"I think we can expect that."

"Shall we call the police?"

CHAPTER 75

"We're not calling anybody."

Gardner went into his library. Against the far wall, below the window, was a credenza he used for storage. He knelt down and opened a sliding door. When he stood he was holding a 9mm handgun and magazine.

"Jesus, no—"

"I don't intend to shoot him," said Gardner. "Just keep him in check. Calm him down."

"He won't be kept in check. And he can't be calmed down."

"Then I hope my aim is as good as it used to be."

"I never should have gotten pregnant."

Headlights streamed across the window. A car swerved into the driveway. It hit one of the garbage cans by the garage door.

"He's here," said Gardner.

Gardner stood. Viola's mother was backing away when Gardner took her by the arm and marched her to the stairs.

"Go up to the apartment on the third floor. Lock the door behind you. Stay there."

Gardner unlocked the front door. Viola's mother stood on the landing wrapped in a wet towel.

"Go on," said Gardner.

"Are you gonna let him in?"

"Of course... now go."

She did as ordered and then Gardner went and sat on the stairs and waited.

He did not have to wait long.

At the same moment that Charlie Dash banged his fist on the

door and shouted Gardner's name, he tried the door with his other hand.

It was open and he bullied his way in. He saw Gardner with a gun on the stairs at the back of the hallway.

Charlie didn't give a damn about the gun and went right for the library, then the office, then the bathroom. He called out to his wife, threatening her. He searched until he was out of breath and out of rooms.

Then there he was in the hall, facing the stairs and his friend.

"Where is she?"

Gardner pointed at the rug where Charlie could see wet footprints going up the stairs, between Gardner's legs, and continuing on to the darkened landing.

CHAPTER 76

"I see you still have your service weapon," said Charlie.

"You were meant to see it."

"I'll bet you haven't cleaned it in years."

"Lawyers tend to be very meticulous."

Gardner saw Charlie was looking very subtly around the hallway.

"Where is the light switch? That's what you're thinking, isn't it, Charlie? Get the room dark, you got a fighting chance."

"She's gonna have to come back."

"If she wants to."

"She might as well abort the baby."

"Go home, Charlie. Go home and count your blessings."

Charlie screamed for his wife to get the hell downstairs. He was talking to the darkness for all the response he got. Then he yelled again, that she would have to come down sometime. Leave the house sometime. Take to the street sometime—

"If you don't leave now," said Gardner, "I'm going to call the police."

"And tell them what? I could leak out enough about you to—"

"And you will get opened up. You're a low end contractor who does clandestine dirty work for the government. While me... I'm just a quiet attorney, with an exclusive clientele. And... it's no accident we both are what we are. Now go home and live with it."

CHAPTER 77

Viola pulled into the Castle driveway. Music playing on her Comet radio. Loud and rocking like she was setting up the night. Headlights staged the front porch where Bill Castle sat waiting and smoking a Kool.

He didn't want to look too anxious so he didn't get up right away. He took a drag on his cigarette first.

She got what he was doing. Playing it cool. She was alright with that. It even fed her ego some.

He came up to the car. She leaned out the window as he hunched down. She felt this nervous pleasure go through her.

She wriggled a finger and in French said, "'Will you come into my car,' said the spider to the fly."

In Spanish he answered back, "I speak Spanish well enough to get the idea of what you said."

In French she answered back, "Monsieur... I am loaded with ideas." Again she wriggled a finger toward the shotgun seat.

He slid across the hood and she was already gunning it out the driveway in reverse as he slid into the front seat.

Matthews Avenue was lined with apartments and it was narrow and she was rifling along.

Bill started to play with the radio dials looking for music that would match the moment.

As she swung onto Pelham Parkway he came across "A Hard Day's Night" and began a drum solo on the dashboard in time to the music. Then she cut into traffic and slipped across lanes and Bill could only shake his head.

"What?" she said.

"I got a case of the awes," he said.

She liked that.

"This is nothing. I learned to drive in Europe. There's no rules in Europe."

CHAPTER 78

There was a tavern in the West Village—the White Horse. It was one of the oldest bars in New York and a lot of famous people over the years hung out there… or at least got consistently drunk there. Bill had never heard of the place.

Viola told him how she'd read about the bar while she was at school in France. She'd put it on her pilgrimage list.

"James Baldwin… Norman Mailer… Dylan Thomas," she said.

Bill didn't know a one of them.

"The poem 'Do Not Go Gentle into That Good Night'… they taught it in school," she said.

"We didn't go gently anywhere," he said. "Except to the principal's office, where they whipped our asses…." He'd lit up another

Kool and smoked away. "I didn't read much after my mother died. I guess I didn't have the temperament for it. School was nothing. I did duke it out with a nun."

As she took the cigarette from him she snaked her fingers over his in one of those little emotion grabber moments.

It was a Saturday night. A balmy night, plenty of car traffic, plenty of foot traffic, plenty of storefront light, plenty of noise and music and the smells of summer. It was one of those nights where there were plenty of sharp lines and secret tunes coming from everywhere.

He thought about telling her of being rejected from the army, but the hell with it. Another time. He was pretty sure what her response would be. The war was strictly thumbs down.

Out of nowhere Bill said, "Think about your mother much?"

He said it with such simple sincerity.

"Not much," Viola said. "Until lately."

"Because of me?"

"Yeah."

"I was a different person once," said Bill.

"You can be a different person again."

"I think about all the conversations I wish I could have had with my mother... but I can't even remember her voice."

They were up on Hudson at a stoplight a couple of blocks from the White Horse. She put the Comet into park and leaned over and kissed him and the moment was captured in a reflection off the windshield. There then gone as the light changed. It was then she said, "Everything is on the move, isn't it?"

CHAPTER 79

The White Horse was an old world tavern. Rough, yes, but still a child of the fifties and early sixties. The patrons were young, hip, and they talked politics and music and movies. They were excited to immerse themselves in all this, to revel in all this. It was a world of expanding the horizons of your mind. It was the world of intellectual immediacy.

It was a place of evolving history and hanging out there, being there, just going there, or passing through there, let you brush up against all that history. History in the making, history happening without you even noticing it.

They had themselves a spot at the bar. Were an image of the eternal imagination, a freewheeling meditation of drinking, lighting each other's cigarettes, soaking in all the chatter and the music and the vibe, even all the pretense that was floating around. And there was that too. Bars like this are never short of pretense.

The real test of uncomplicated youth is uncomplicated youth. Which is running away from you the closer you get to it. But put all that aside, they had no idea how much of their own lives was bringing them together, that each of their histories would come to be central to the other's very existence, as if they had been joined together even before birth.

They were both drunkish and he thought it time to unburden himself and tell her about the letter and he leaned down and whispered, "I got rejected from the army."

She looked up. He waited to see how she would take this. She was elated, not wanting to see him killed in a pointless war, but something warned her not to express any such emotion. That this had been something very important to him, and wild enthusiasm over it not working out was not the way to go. It also told her how much she already cared for him.

"I'm sorry," she said. "What happened?"

He took the folded letter from his jeans pocket and shook it loose. She saw it had a lot of holes in it.

"Knife holes," he said.

While she read the government letter a folk singer in the back room started in playing "The Times They Are a-Changin'" and invited everyone to join in.

Protest anthems against the war were the thing there. The more the songs gave you a taste of the politics of the day, the better the crowd liked it.

Peter, Paul, and Mary; Pete Seeger; Joan Baez; Bob Dylan... the patrons knew the lyrics to their songs like they knew the names of family members.

It got loud in that streetcorner tavern. The voices filled up the space big time. And there was a righteous fervor you could hear halfway up the block.

"What's it mean?" said Viola.

Bill couldn't hear her and cupped a hand over his ear.

"What's it mean?" she said, pointing at the letter.

"It means I got the thumbs down."

"No... for your health... long term... Is your heart okay?"

"Oh, yeah," he said. "The doctor told me it was good enough to be broken any number of times."

She looked him over with a real cutting concern.

"You're not trying to sneak around the truth, are you?"

"Let's get out of here," he said, and he took her by the arm. Suddenly, to her, he seemed much older.

CHAPTER 80

They slipped out of the White Horse and into a Saturday night on Hudson Street where in one of those perfect arm in arm postcard images they cruised over to Washington Square.

You could smell the weed now in the summer air. Kids on stoops, or lording down the sidewalks in packs, hipster college kids with good old fashioned joints, all very cool and stoned. Viola pointed to a radio in a parked car playing a Four Seasons song.

"The Four Seasons. I saw them in England."

"What's your favorite Four Seasons song?"

She thought a bit. "'Big Man in Town.' Yours?"

"'Ragdoll.'"

"They all laughed at her, didn't they?" said Viola.

"How 'bout Motown?" said Bill. "I love Motown."

"The Four Tops… the best," said Viola.

"The Temptations… 'My Girl,'" he said.

"I prefer 'My Guy.'"

They passed a bookstore with a huge cutout of Shakespeare in the window.

"Check that out. What do you think about 'Romeo and Juliet'?" she said.

"I don't know the play… but the Reflections I know."

"Romeo had a little job to do, didn't he?" She flashed a ring finger.

"As long as they avoid all those Romeo and Juliet tragedies," he said.

"I saw the Reflections," she said, "in a Roy Orbison rock bands concert."

"'It's Over'… Great song. Orbison is better than Elvis."

"Elvis *is* God."

"What song do you like better... 'Blowin' in the Wind' or 'Cast Your Fate to the Wind'?" she said.

He hummed a few bars of "Cast Your Fate."

She bit his neck. "That was to get your attention."

He bit her neck back. "You got it."

"'Mister Tambourine Man,'" she said.

"What about it?"

"Acoustic or electric?"

"You mean Dylan or the Byrds?"

"I mean exactly that."

"The Byrds... 100 percent."

They began a riff of their favorites, doing a one up.

"Let it be me," she said.

"Don't worry, baby," he said.

"Beach Boys... I saw them in England. How 'bout 'Don't Let the Sun Catch You Crying' by Jerry and the Peacemakers?"

"How 'bout anything by the Beatles?"

"How 'bout the Stones?"

"Satisfaction, baby. I could use a little of that right now," he said.

She grabbed him and did a number on his neck and chest. "And how's that for girlie action?"

"And then, man, did she kiss me."

"The Chiffons," she said. "The Shirelles, the Ronettes' 'Be My Baby'... The Shangri-Las... The girl bands, honey boy... Giving out all the love they have."

He bit her on the neck again.

"Paul and Paula," he said.

"'Hey Paula'... One of the all time greats," she said. "That's the way love should be."

"A total heartbanger."

"Chubby Checker doing the Twist," she said.

"'The Twist'… Or 'Let's Twist Again'?"

"Ohhh… that's a coin toss."

CHAPTER 81

On their way to Washington Square they crossed over Bedford Street, which was where Mike Malone had his offices and Viola was set to meet with him to discuss the "internship," if you could call it that.

81 Bedford Street was the exact address, and it was a few doors down from Chumley's Pub, which at one time had been a notorious speakeasy for the West Village art crowd. It had catered for years to the Beatniks and the Beat Generation and whatever Generation would come in next in all likelihood. It was also a place where Malone and the agents who worked clandestinely with the government would meet to plot and relax.

And Viola would come to learn that no place could be a better exemplar of the dichotomy that was America.

CHAPTER 82

Washington Square Park, beyond its iconic arch, was a hotbed of activity on weekends. You had street poets doing their street poet thing and painters doing their painter thing. You had social protestors and philosophizers doing their social protestor and philosophizer thing.

There were students from NYU and City College and everyday New Yorkers and tourists. And there was music. That night the

Village Stompers were playing. They were a hipster Dixieland jazz band that had had the number one hit in America the previous year, titled, of all things, "Washington Square."

On the way there they bought a bottle of Bacardi and a mixer of Coke and hustled some space on a bench by the pond from a mishmash of City College freshmen, swapping hits of rum for tokes on a joint and a piece of that bench. Then Viola bought one of those Clint Eastwood *Fistful of Dollars* cigarillos from a chick who was passing by. Topping that she swapped another shot of rum for a Polaroid from a guy taking snapshots.

They were getting good and settled in, her on his lap, he with his arm snaked between her thighs, those little physical moments like beautifully laid out sentences, when here comes an army of protestors, black, white, Spanish, passing out fliers, talking up the Voting Rights Act.

One of the fliers was exactly the same as the one she had been handed earlier and the whole crazy day came to her, the whole thing in her head about her father coming back to her.

She leaned into Bill's shoulder. The smells of fresh soap and pot.

"I need to ask you something," said Viola.

"Yeah?"

"Do I look Puerto Rican to you?"

"You are Puerto Rican."

"But do I look Puerto Rican?"

"I don't get it."

"I don't think my father loves me. I'm not sure if he even likes me. Is connected to me as a human being. And I think it's about me being Puerto Rican."

Then Bill said something, off the top of his head, actually, that wrenched the hell out of her.

They were close together on that bench, utterly alone in a crowd, when he came out with "Maybe it's you."

"What?"

"Maybe you can't accept the fact that you are Puerto Rican. That you're angry or ashamed because of what you are. And your feelings have nothing to do really with your father at all."

Her look stopped him dead.

She stood. He did not understand. She searched through her shoulder bag, found her keys, and flipped them to him.

"Go back home," she said. "I'll catch up with you later."

He hadn't wanted to let her go, but she was intense. Not mad at him, but severe.

"Was I wrong?" he said. "I'm sorry if I was … it's what I felt."

CHAPTER 83

Bill pulled into the driveway. Warsh saw the headlights fan across the ceiling and went to the window to see. Bill got out of the girl's car… but no girl.

Warsh opened the window and leaned out. "You come home with the girl's car… but not the girl."

"That about sums it up, Papi."

"Most men would say you got the better end of the deal."

Bill took a Kool from his shirt pocket and lit up.

"You two have a fight?"

"She had a fight."

"With who?"

"With herself."

THE IMAGINARY BOY

CHAPTER 84

Later that Saturday night Mike Malone was nearing the end of a long debriefing of the priest who had been brought in from Laos by Warsh and Charlie Dash.

They were working out of a secured apartment at 81 Bedford Street. The building itself was a six story brick apartment. Very classy, very low key. The perfect safe house for the evil that men do.

The priest had been brought to the States because he knew of a vast network of underground supply depots and military shelters set up in the jungles by the communists, where they could wage a clandestine and on the move war against the United States.

One of the apartment bedrooms served as a command post, with a bare card table, overseas phones, and walls consumed with photos of the location and matching Laotian maps.

Charlie Dash and Warsh were in Malone's living room, drinking beer, eating cold pizza, and watching *Gunsmoke*. The capper was that both were wearing their sidearms.

"A loser's Saturday night," said Charlie. "If I say so myself."

"It could be worse," said Warsh, breaking off a crusty and cold pizza slice. We could have wives to deal with."

Warsh saw how restless Charlie was. How that little statement of fact affected him.

"They're out together... deal with it," said Warsh.

"And if they seriously hook up?"

"Give them a chance. They may grow to hate each other. But... if it has to get ugly, I'll deal with it," said Warsh.

CHAPTER 85

Malone came out of the back bedroom and closed the door behind him. The priest was sitting at a card table, his fingers pressed to his temples.

"How'd it go in there?" said Charlie.

"He's one wiped out Catholic," said Malone.

"Did he prove to be valuable?"

"Two weeks… very valuable. He knows more than most of our military personnel," said Malone.

"What's he doing?" said Charlie.

"Praying," said Malone.

"That's something we don't often have a use for," said Warsh.

"Fuck you," said Charlie.

Malone went to the fridge and retrieved himself a beer. A minute later the priest came up the hallway. He looked exhausted. He knocked off a few sentences in French.

"He's saying hello," said Malone. "Said he hopes your boys are well."

Warsh gave him a thumbs up.

Malone offered him the beer.

The *Gunsmoke* episode caught the priest's eye and he watched the episode with acute interest. There was Matt Dillon, sheriff of Dodge City, in a standard issue television gunfight. It made the priest smile. He actually mimicked Matt Dillon drawing his gun. He took the beer, he drank, he looked at the bottle. His face had a series of emotions pass over it. He stood there in the room and began to talk.

It was in French, so Malone had to translate. The priest wanted to know if they were done with him. And if so, he'd like to return to Laos.

Malone reminded the priest they had broached this subject before, in all its complications, and he'd been advised, warned really, returning home might well be signing his death warrant. That for his patriotic act against the communists he would face unspeakable torture.

This the priest knew. He had broken his sovereign vows of Christianity by involving himself in the war. He thought of the Martyrs of Laos. This much he could say in English—the Martyrs of Laos—who had been murdered for their faith by refusing to conform or take part in violence. And so, he wanted to return to his homeland to atone for his sins, even if those sins were for a righteous cause.

Charlie called him a fool, and worse. "Stay the fuck here and live a life" pretty much summarized it.

The priest had no idea what Charlie had said and looked to Malone, who in English said, "I have no intention of telling him that... and neither will you."

Warsh, on the other hand, had taken a Saint Christopher's from around his neck and he slipped it into the priest's hand. This the priest understood.

"We will see, in time," said Malone in French, "how to get you home safely."

Of course Malone knew, as did the others, that this was not on his dance card.

CHAPTER 86

About four in the morning came a softly celestial knock at Bill's front door. He was crashed out on the couch in the dark. So no answer.

Viola went to knock again when an upstairs window opened.

She eased back and looked up to see an unhappy Warsh leaning out the window.

"Sorry," she said, "if I woke you, but—"

"The door," he whispered. "The note on the door. No need to knock. The note."

"What note?" she said.

She looked at the door. And there it was, tacked to the door. Right in her eyeline. Impossible to miss.

She pulled it loose. Read it.

Let yourself in. I'm asleep on the couch.

She held it out so Warsh could see she found it.

"How'd I miss it?" she said.

CHAPTER 87

She opened the door and stepped into the house quiet as a cat. She took off her boots and put them on the table in the foyer. She also carefully took off the necklace and beads she wore on her wrist and set them aside.

She moved along slowly in the house as her bearings were not good but she found him eventually in a wash of light through the front window blinds.

He had taken off his shoes and socks and shirt and was stretched out on his back and she thought how she could just stare at that rough vision of him and what her mind could do with it.

She sat across from that sleeping youth, watching his chest rise and fall. A slight island of light from that streetlamp just about where his heart would be.

She looked over the darkened room. She hadn't noticed before, everything in there was old—couch, coffee table, breakfront, rugs.

All bought back in the fifties, probably from when his mother was alive. Clearance sale furniture. Maybe Macy's of Parkchester. Furniture that gave you the illusion of upward mobility, but also touched one's sense of pride.

Her life had never touched this life. Her world had never touched this world. Her life and world had been privileged. The schools she went to in Europe let her live better than ninety five percent of the people in the world.

She'd gotten a dose of revelation from that sleeping youth, which is what she intended to tell him. How in the back of her mind she always carried around resentment that her father didn't really care for her as a birth father would. That she was in some way a token, and this fostered a disquiet.

She had gone up to Spanish Harlem after leaving Bill. She walked the streets there. The poor streets where people lived, just barely. These were the people and the streets that, if it were not for her being adopted, might have well been her legacy. She had no wish to be one with that and she wondered if Bill sensed this feeling hidden within her. Because the more true it was, the less right she had to blame her father.

CHAPTER 88

Something woke him... her breathing most likely. She had stood up and he saw her now, her outline anyway. As the sleep fell away she had begun to undress. First her Indian shirt, then her lean dark arms slipped out of her bra.

"Thank you," she said.

"For what?"

"You see the world through your own eyes… or you see yourself through the world's eyes."

"Where'd that come from?"

"You… sort of."

She slipped out of her jean shorts, and then her underpants. Her thick dark hair went perfectly with her black stockings.

"You want me to undress you?" she said. "Or would you rather I just watch?"

The light through the window was just enough for her to see his white teeth as he smiled.

CHAPTER 89

The address Viola was to go to was 81 Bedford Street in Manhattan. It was not the second floor apartment where the priest was being kept for his debriefing. This apartment was on the first floor, just off from the lobby, and served as Mike Malone's formal office and living quarters.

When she arrived he sat her down at the dining table and offered her coffee. He was collegiate and professional. He was sincere, and gave off a vibe of absolute trust. He was, you might say, a consummate agent—or a man of discerning lies.

Viola took it all in. She had been introduced by her father to professionals like this. There was a plaque Charlie Dash kept on his desk: *Watch silently, listen carefully.* A reminder to himself, you might say.

She'd brought her college admission papers as Malone had requested. Her "internship" would go through the summer to the end of the first semester. She was on probation until class started.

Her job was to attend rallies and protests for the Voting Rights Act. She was to listen and watch and keep good notes about anyone or any group that fostered the idea of violence or sabotage. Youth organizations were of particular interest. She was not to join any group, even if invited, but seek Malone's advice on how to proceed.

At the end of the interview Malone asked Viola if she was going to inform her father of the internship.

She had decided against that.

Malone wanted to know why.

"I want to earn my way… I want him to know I've done it, when I've done it."

CHAPTER 90

Bill was leaning over the engine of a Buick Special putting in new plugs. And after last night he was working on borrowed energy, at best, when what does he hear?

"How would you like to change your life?"

He came out from under the hood. He hadn't seen her since just before dawn when she left the house on Matthews Avenue to change. She was just getting back from her meeting with Mr. Malone. She wore a simple Lord and Taylor dress and a pair of Mary Janes. She smelled of sandalwood, which turned him on very much.

"You look very—"

"Magazine cover, right?" she said. "It's all a fraud."

They kissed each other hard. The real trick was keeping all that engine scrunge and oil off her clothes. She saw one of Bill's gas pump attendants was checking them out. She gave him a thumbs up sign and he turned away just this side of embarrassed.

"Well," she said. "How would you like to change your life?"

"For better or for worse?"

"Not sure… it could go either way."

CHAPTER 91

There was a luncheonette about walking distance down White Plains Road. It was right under the elevated so the eating joint was never short of the shrill grind of trainwheels.

It was also a place Bill came to often with his mother though he did not mention it. Viola assumed as much, and did not dig into the subject. And she still had not confessed to Bill about the personal ad she had put in the Bronx newspapers.

CHAPTER 92

"So," said Bill. "Here we are."

"Here we are," she answered.

He had grease on his face which she cleaned off with a napkin she'd wetted and so she began about Malone and the meeting.

When she finished, and she finished rather quickly, Bill said, "It was just like that? That simple."

"That simple. Short as a quiz."

"You know what's doing."

"I want you to tell me what you think he's doing."

"It's the smooth recruitment."

"You mean he's trying to turn me into people like your Papi, or my father."

Bill shook his head. "I don't know how much we get into that... for our own sakes."

"How much is there?"

"You're gonna open the door," said Bill.

"Am I?"

"Yeah."

"Is that what you think?"

"Yeah."

"Haven't you ever wondered if there might come a time where we compare notes?"

"You thought about that?"

"Haven't you?"

"There's a lot of things I think about... I don't do."

"And not because you're afraid."

CHAPTER 93

"Because I know where you have to take this," he said. "It's like blowing over the Berlin Wall."

"But you're prepared, right? The gun?"

"What gun?"

"The one tucked down in your jeans."

She'd reached under the table and tapped his groin where he always kept that small menacing Walther 22, ready and willing.

"You're breathing trouble," he said.

"Am I? I don't mean to be."

"That's always the way. People that don't mean to be are the ones, in the end, that mean to be."

For a moment it looked as if her whole body frowned.

CHAPTER 94

Bill shook his head. Deadly, he thought. Then he began to riff out a few bars of Ricky Nelson's hit record *Fools Rush In*.

"How would you like to ask me what you think I'm doing?"

"I'm not sure I want to do that."

"Not curious?"

"Worse."

He got up. Went to the register and paid for a couple of cups of coffee. He went out the door with her trailing behind him saying, "I didn't come here with no plan in mind."

The train was passing overhead and then there was that ear piercing screech as it pulled into the station. A perfect counterpoint to this conversation.

"And I mean here… back home."

They got caught up in the crowd at the corner waiting for the light. He thought of sprinting it, but she'd be right on him.

"I came here to find out the truth of things."

"What the hell are you talking about? The truth of what things?"

The light changed.

CHAPTER 95

She crossed the street, walking quickly. He followed now.

The fatal mistake is asking the right question in the same question.

She went back to the gas station. She bummed a Kool from him. She leaned back against the hood of her car and smoked.

"You, dear sir," she said, "know exactly what I'm talking about. You know more than me, probably, living here as long as you have, seeing all you have, picking up, hearing, eavesdropping on things like you might have. The College of Criminal Justice… I came here to find out about me… us… our families. You and I come out of the same well. And it's no wishing well."

He lit a Kool for himself. He started to walk around her car, thinking, thinking, thinking, scuffing at the asphalt. She was in his head and she knew it.

"I want to find out who I am… and who you are is part of who I am, like I'm a part of who you are. I want to see what's doing in this country… and our people… and write it down.

"It was the soft recruitment, like you called it," she said, "happening in Mr. Malone's office. But it wasn't him doing the soft recruitment."

CHAPTER 96

"Oh man," he said. "Where do you carry your scythe? 'Cause I don't see it."

She tapped the side of her head.

"In here," she said.

He could only stare.

"You wear a nice dress and a pair of friendly shoes that don't make you look too tall. It's all in the bedside manner," she said.

He came up alongside her. He leaned back against her car.

"Do I need to keep an eye on you?" he said.

"I wrote you a letter."

"What?"

"I wrote you a letter."

"I never got any letter."

"I never sent it… yet."

"I don't understand."

"I wrote it to a boy. The boy was you. Only I didn't call you by your name. You were… The Imaginary Boy."

She crossed her arms. She was looking off. Bill wondered at what, where.

"I wrote it over a bunch of years," she said. "Adding to it. The Imaginary Boy helped me get through years of loneliness in Europe. Years of unhappiness. Years of having no family. No one to share dreams with. The Imaginary Boy listened to all that and he was the boy in the beautiful blue Lincoln."

She looked wounded, fawnlike, someone who understood and felt what it's like to be deeply unloved.

"I'm not crazy," she said. "I'm not malicious. I'm not dangerous. At least I think I'm not."

CHAPTER 97

Gardner Flynn, the attorney, had been fielding correspondence to the ad from people claiming to have pertinent information regarding the Mary Buergos murder. Of course, they were mostly con artists, flakes, scammers, people desperate for a handout. Their stories were inexhaustible and exhausting. Until he received a letter from a priest in a chapel in, of all places, the Bergen Mall.

The Bergen Mall was the first suburban mall in New Jersey. It opened in 1957—the same year as the murder. It was where John F.

Kennedy announced his run for the presidency. Besides thousands of square feet of shops it had a legitimate theatre, a bowling alley, kiddie amusement rides, and its own post office. People came from New York to shop and beat the high New York taxes. On the lower floor was a western town which was a hallway of small shops. And at the end of that long hallway was a chapel where the liturgical services took place three times a day.

Gardner called Viola for her to come to his office, take the letter, read it, and then discuss it with him, if she thought that would be worthwhile.

She arrived alone, and before Gardner could address the fact Bill was not there, she said, "I haven't told him yet. But yet is getting pretty close."

Gardner handed her the letter. It was a large envelope, and sealed. She looked at Gardner when she realized there was another, smaller envelope inside the outer one. A copy of the personal ad was taped to the outside and so was a handwritten note that read:

Dear Father Orteig,

Please see the envelope within is passed on to the appropriate parties.

CHAPTER 98

The priest had taken on the task. He'd even left a number where Gardner could reach him at the chapel.

The envelope within the envelope had a simple note included:

I believe the man who committed the murder was someone I dated a short time back in 1957. If you care to meet, leave a note on the chapel bulletin board. Also—proceed with caution. He ran with an unsavory crowd.

After reading the note she passed it to Gardner. As was his way he read and reread and reread the few sentences with long reflective pauses in between.

"What do you think?" she said.

"I feel… it falls into one of two categories. Very well done scam… or troubling possibility."

She felt a little frightened suddenly.

"And I don't like the fact that they used the word 'unsavory,'" he said.

"What about it?"

"It's not the kind of word some uneducated kook would use."

"You mean it fits better with someone educated."

"Yes."

"Does it make you think this is more the 'troubling possibility' than the 'scam.'"

"Yes."

"Well," said Viola, "I have to find out either way."

"I don't think you've thought this through."

"I'm going to drive out to Jersey."

"The chapel."

"Yes."

"Not alone."

"I won't be alone."

"You're going to tell Bill. That way—"

"The priest."

"Bill has a right to know. Doesn't he?"

"He also has a right to say no. Which I don't want him to do."

CHAPTER 99

When she left Gardner's office she headed straight for the George Washington Bridge and Route 4 to Paramus and the Bergen Mall. The chapel was, like she'd been told, at the far end of the basement hallway, past the shops with their Dodge City fronts. It was, she thought, the full shot glass of irony.

The chapel was quite something in its simplicity. An altar, flanked by holy statuary, a few dozen seats, a wall of red devotional candles, a table at the entry with religious pamphlets, a bulletin board, all of it under flat fluorescent lighting.

Mass was happening. A priest was administering communion. He was a bulky older man. She wondered if it was Father Orteig.

She went and tacked a note to the bulletin board.

Received your letter. Will be here tomorrow.

She then went and sat in the back row and waited for the mass to end.

CHAPTER 100

After the mass the dozen or so parishioners slipped back into their lives and Viola introduced herself to the priest.

"I'm Viola Dash. Are you Father Orteig?"

"Ahhh." He was a congenial man who took her by the hand. "You received the envelope."

"Yes… Thank you… Can I ask you a few questions?"

He had a goodbye or two to say. He knew many of the people by name so Viola assumed most were regular parishioners.

There was a small office partitioned off from the chapel by golden drapery where he had her sit. He closed the drapes so they could have some expectation of privacy.

"I assume the envelope was self explanatory?" said Viola.

"Yes."

"I see the people who come, you know most of them. Do you know the person who gave you that note?"

The priest became suddenly officious. "I'm sorry, but I can't answer that."

"Why not?"

"It was given to me during confession."

"Does the woman come here often? Has she come here often?"

"I can't answer that for the very same reason."

Viola thought how she might get past his apostolic answers.

"Do you think it's safe for me to proceed?" said Viola.

"How do I answer," said Father Orteig, "something I cannot answer." He considered his situation. "Are you Catholic?"

"I'm adopted. My parents were Puerto Rican. Or so I'm told."

"And your adopted family?"

"My mother is dead. My father… in no way does he have faith like the people here today."

"Do you have faith?" said the priest.

It was the first time in years that she had been addressed with such a question.

"Why are you here?" said Father Orteig.

"Here?"

"The woman told me about the murder. I saw the newspaper. Why are you doing this?"

"I want... the young man... his mother was the one who was murdered. I'd like to see him have his life back."

"Could it be that you're trying to get your own life back? Your own faith in life back?"

"I don't know," she said.

"Could you be chasing your own faith?"

She was momentarily overwhelmed.

"It may not be safe for you to go forward. But it will be right," he said. "And let us not be weary in doing good, for at the proper time we will reap a harvest if we do not give up... St. Paul."

CHAPTER 101

They talked for maybe a polite minute more. Father Orteig told her she was always welcome and that he was available to her at any time, and then Viola left.

But something on the way out of the chapel caught her eye. The note—it was gone.

She looked around. There were only two people in the chapel—a man sitting alone, praying, and a woman lighting a candle.

Viola hurried out. Down the long hallway a half dozen shoppers came and went.

Whoever had sent the letter had been there. What are the odds of that? Had the person been making a daily pilgrimage to the chapel, waiting? Deciding on how to handle this, seeing what kind of threat Viola might be. Or what kind of fool.

CHAPTER 102

Somebody had taken the note from the bulletin board while she was there. Somebody had a point to make, and made it. But what was it, and who was it, and why was it being done this way?

Viola walked the long hallway of tiny western fronted shops to the elevator. She'd been seen. She'd been seen and looked over. She'd been seen, looked over and studied, evaluated, sized up, judged. The list could go on from the benign to the threatening.

Not good news no matter how you explain it.

She stopped and pretended to look in a shop window. But it was nothing but an opportunity to steal a glance back toward the chapel to see if she was being followed.

There was an alcove with a single elevator and an open stairwell to the main floor. She pressed for the elevator. When the door opened she entered and as the door closed a hand reached in and the door opened again.

A woman entered. Viola stole a look. The woman could have been forty, maybe. She was lean, starkfaced. Her skin was pale and short on makeup. Viola was so caught up in the woman she had forgotten to press the button on the main floor. As she and the woman were the only ones on the elevator the woman leaned past her and pressed the button herself.

CHAPTER 103

They existed in that elevator for an otherwise nothing passage of time with Viola thinking—*Is this the one? Am I being hunted down, confronted, or is this something else?*

Just as the elevator settled into the main floor, but before the doors had opened, a conflicted, uncertain Viola, out of nowhere, said to this stranger woman, "June nineteenth... nineteen fifty seven."

The woman had seen Viola say something and she answered in a fractured, incomplete voice, "I am... har... a hearing. Please look at me and speak clearly and slowly... I will ansa."

IF NOT THE MONEY, THEN WHAT?

CHAPTER 104

The moment took her over. She would never have suspected—

"I'm sorry," said Viola. "I thought you were someone else."

The excuse felt stupid and weak. It felt like a lie.

She hurried out of the elevator and out of the mall and into the parking lot riding a wave of confusion, cursing herself for a self imposed humiliation.

She momentarily forgot where she parked her car and stood in the tortuous Jersey sun trying to get her act together.

Once in the car she sat there banging her open hands against the steering wheel. The inside of the car was hot, so hot from the weather. She was sweating. She opened the windows.

She kept telling herself—get your head together. Get calm. Ask yourself questions—answer the questions. If you can. Concentrate. What if that woman had been the right person, why didn't she just come out and say something? Was she sizing up Viola, could that be it? Could she have followed Viola out into the parking lot?

Viola began to scan the rows of parked cars, the sun glaring off their hoods. Impossible to find her now. But be found—or followed.

Could all this have been a trap to lure Viola into the open? She started up the Comet. She sped out of the lot and onto Route 4 toward the George Washington Bridge. Her heart was racing. She actually was overwhelmed with a sense she was being followed, and overwhelmed at the same time this was just a state of paranoia.

She kept watching the rearview all the while, topping the speed limit, seeing what might be back there. She even pulled off the highway and into a huge furniture store parking lot. Then she exited at the far end of the street. Nothing looked to be out of the ordinary, but she kept imagining the murderer of Bill's mother lurking over her shoulder and she couldn't sweat it out of her mind.

CHAPTER 105

Viola decided to confer with Gardner Flynn. He'd been expecting her anyway to give him the play by play. She needed now to get his sage opinion.

He took it all in. His first comment: "Don't you think at this point, Bill should be told?"

"After tomorrow," said Viola. "If something happens tomorrow. If you think I should go at all."

He had a few brief thoughts on the matter. Thoughts that had him staring into a faceless empty coffee cup, like he was looking for magic. "They know who you are, right... by now. They could have taken down your license plate after you left the chapel. They could have followed you here." He ran an index finger over his lower lip. "It may not be the money they're after."

"If not the money, then what?"

"Finding out what kind of threat you pose."

CHAPTER 106

They were sharing a tub with a rising mountain of bubbles. No lights—please. Just a few candles around the edges of the room, dramatically placed so every look, every physical nuance created a couple of extra shadows. And there's nothing like shadows, extra or otherwise.

Bill got them music from his stereo in the bedroom. Viola rubbed his stomach with the bottom of her dark, smooth foot.

"Rubbing your lantern I think I'm getting my first wish."

"It's magic alright," he said.

"Will you still love me," she whispered.

"Tomorrow?" he answered. "But tonight—"

"Completely... I need completely," she said.

"What's that look in your eye?"

"It's love, baby."

"Can I believe—"

She held her hand to her chest. It's those unspoken words, like the ones happening now.

He lifted her foot out of the bubbles and kissed it. She was ecstatic, and then she wasn't, and then he saw the shift.

"What is it?" he said.

"What?" she said.

"There's something going on behind that sweet expression."

"What makes you say that?"

"We were together one minute and then… you disappeared."

"Maybe it's just… I'm afraid we might lose this."

She was lying. She was back in New Jersey, at the mall, in the chapel.

CHAPTER 107

Viola rose up out of the tub… covered in bubbles. A Bronx vision of *Madonna on the Half Shell.* She danced around the bathroom to a song that just came on the stereo.

Barbara Lewis… "Baby, I'm Yours."

She loved the song. Ever since she first heard it in a funky Paris bar. It was a secret theme song of her emotions.

She glided out into the hallway. Forsaken and wanton. Who could leave her alone like that? No one sane, anyway. Bill eased out of the tub closing in on that crowned jewel of a chick and slid his arm around her, his tongue across her nipples. The bubbles between them dripping to the floor.

You couldn't list all that was cool about this for them and her with bubbles in her hair like a queen's crown.

"I'll be yours, baby," she said.

"You mean like the song says?"

"I mean like the song says… only better… better, better, better."

All of this in that dazzling nowhere of a hallway with the shadows from the candles through the open bathroom door and their feet leaving wet dancing footprints on the floor.

She pointed to the floor. "Are we gonna be like those footprints… there for a time, then gone?"

"Oh," he said. "Longer than that."

She left a string of kisses down his neck.

"How long?" she said.

"At least as long as—"

Viola screamed out.

A fist was smashing against the front porch window.

"Holy shit," she said.

It was her father, and man, was he cursing them out. With a voice like a locomotive, no less.

Bill ran up the hall naked.

Charlie was demanding they open the fuckin' door.

Bill grabbed a baseball bat he kept beside the breakfront and began hitting the ceiling with it.

Viola ran into the bathroom and grabbed a towel. She knocked over some candles in the process. The light went crazy.

Charlie was trying to smash his way in.

CHAPTER 108

The front door was coming off its hinges.

With baseball bat in hand Bill yelled, pleaded, for her father to can it.

Viola was ordering her father to go, holding the bath towel tight against her, shivering now, the carpet soaked, the tracks of their footprints a ruined confusion.

In a bath towel she thought, "I'm here begging my father. God help me."

The door ripped loose.

Who the fuck screamed? Was it Viola? Was it her father?

Bill was banging the top of the bat on the ceiling with an SOS signal for Papi that he'd been taught as a kid years before.

Talk about fierceness, Charlie heaved himself at the door like a total bull.

Viola was begging her father to stop.

Bill held the bat up ready to deliver some real violence.

"Don't hurt him!" Viola shouted.

Charlie was just coming through the door when Warsh grabbed him from the back.

Charlie reeked with booze.

He was cursing out his daughter, he was cursing out Bill.

Warsh got him to his knees.

Bill threw the bat aside and jumped Charlie.

He and Warsh wrestled Viola's drunken father to the ground. He was running off at the mouth, calling his daughter some ugly shit.

The worst for her—when he called her a fuckin' Puerto Rican cunt.

Warsh told her to get her clothes and be outta there.

She ran to the bedroom and scooped up her stuff.

She dropped one shoe—forget it.

Her father tried to grab her leg as she leapt over him.

She made it to the car and there she was naked, wet, speeding up Matthews Avenue. The things he'd said to her resonating in her head.

CHAPTER 109

She was at the chapel the next morning as the note she'd left said she would.

She sat in a pew chair, quiet, unhappy, angry, and lost.

A hand came to rest on her shoulder.

She looked up to see it was the priest.

"You look like you're shouldering the world this morning."

"Not the world, Father. Just a couple of continents."

"Large continents… or small continents?"

"Sensitive *and* with a sense of humor. That is being blessed."

"May I sit?"

"Please, Father."

"Would you like to talk, or just have the quiet comfort of someone?"

She paused a moment, mouth dry.

"I'm adopted," she said. "I'm Puerto Rican. My father, who is not, called me some dark racial insults."

The priest rubbed his fingers on the chair back, thinking, moving his head from side to side. "You'd think people would realize there are already enough wounds to go around."

"So how do I deal with it?" she said.

"We are all born into innocence, and we are all destinated to lose it."

"And what's left?" said Viola. "The brute hurts we bear?"

"We are left with… forgiveness. Because it will come in handy for all of us… over time."

CHAPTER 110

She waited out the day in the chapel, her father's words in one ear and the priest's in the other. A classic harbinger of human conflicts.

The hours passed—and nothing.

Mass began, mass ended—and nothing.

Viola went to the bathroom, lit up a joint, chugged down a beer, came back to the chapel—and nothing.

At the end of the day she walked the length of the hall to the elevator, despondent. Her insides in the full state of the blues.

She waited with two other women. As they boarded, the doors closed and a hand reached in.

There she was. The woman from the day before.

She said nothing. She did not look at Viola.

CHAPTER 111

As they exited the elevator the women went their ways. The one from the day before who was near deaf passed close by Viola, but did not look at her, not a penny's worth of acknowledgment.

Viola just stood there. She did not know what to make of this, or what to do next. If anything.

Viola reached into her shoulder bag for a cigarette, and what does she find?

An envelope. And written on it—June 19, 1957.

She turned and looked into the crowd where the near deaf woman had gone. She might as well have been a ghost.

Viola did not open the envelope until she was in her car in the parking lot.

In it were a few handwritten pages.

> *Your first question, I'm sure, is how did I get this envelope in your shoulder bag. I am a pickpocket. That is how I make my living. That is how I made my living in 1957.*
>
> *I go by the name of Beonca Costa.*

She then went on to confess, in detail, how she worked in the subways and upscale bars, targeting well to do men. Men in expensive suits, older men well off, intoxicated men were a special source of victim.

In 1957, she'd hoisted a wallet from a guy on the BMT. It turned out he'd had a real bankroll on him. Almost eleven hundred dollars. But there was also something else—

He also had a half dozen driver's licenses. All under different names. And from different states. He had business cards to match. He even had one as a retired naval officer.

If we proceed, she wrote, and come to a "financial decision" that works for both of us I will make everything I have available.

> *I can't promise he is the guy who committed the murder, but I did learn that he was part of a much broader network of disguised criminality. Because it also became part of my life.*
>
> *By the way, I am not deaf or hard of hearing. I was only being cautious.*

There was risk, she wrote, he was not the murderer but he had admitted to it in a drug induced state and that it had been a horrible mistake.

CHAPTER 112

Warsh got a call. It was Mike Malone. He was in a stark mood. They talked a brief minute, but it was long enough.

Charlie was crashed out at Warsh's. He looked like something laid to rest in that storage bedroom.

Warsh shook him to wake him. No luck. Warsh had to resort to slapping Charlie's face.

He was one drunked out middle aged man with a bad attitude. He'd only managed to get his pants halfway off the night before.

Charlie came to, sort of.

"What?" he said, his head meandering loosely in the dark.

Charlie was trying to find Warsh, who by now had opened the blinds. The room filled with a punishing daylight.

"I'm awake," said Charlie. "For whatever that's worth."

"Malone called."

"Yeah?"

"He was looking for you, but settled for me."

"Seniority… Well… here I am."

Warsh stood by the window. Charlie half sat up.

"He's got a problem."

Charlie made a deep grunting sound.

"Somebody we used to know, turns out, is still alive."

This got the blood moving through Charlie's clogged arteries.

"Who says this?"

"Frankie Avalon."

"That dago. Is he sure?"

"Sure is gonna be when we are sure."

"Who is it, by the way?"

"Nat Blue."

"Where was he spotted?"

"Upstate... Lake George."

"I hate Lake George."

CHAPTER 113

Charlie lifted himself from the bed like he was living out the labors of Hercules.

Warsh heard boots coming up the stairs. Knew it was Bill. Told Charlie, "Don't incite trouble."

No sooner had Charlie said, "What do you mean?", when Bill framed up in the doorway and Charlie knew.

He and Warsh both saw Bill was holding a handgun at his side to complete the picture.

"What do I see there?" said Charlie. "A man with a purpose."

"Put that away," said Warsh.

Bill told Charlie, "You ever try and muscle your way into my house again—"

Warsh shouted, "Put it away!"

Bill said, "I smoke your ass."

"This is my house," said Warsh. "You hear me, boy?"

"Just making a point, Papi."

He then slid the automatic under his shirt and into his belt.

"And what you said about your daughter... Worse than disgraceful. You need a real roughing up for that."

Charlie went to stand, tottered a bit with his murderous hangover. He still had only one leg in his pants and did he look a fool.

"I'll shock the hell out of you, kid... I deserve a lot worse, and my reckoning will come. I'll probably even see to it myself."

He started to cry. He covered his face and slumped back down on the bed. A total washout.

Warsh told Bill, "Get out… Leave us here."

Bill turned to leave. "After all these years. He's the best you can do for a friend."

"Friendship comes in a lot of shades and a lot of colors," said Warsh. "But it doesn't come with any warning on the label."

CHAPTER 114

Viola had called Bill and asked they hook up at Gardner's office. Bill knew without asking something was off, like a windy day in hell.

She waited for him in the second floor apartment that Gardner used for a variety of circumstances. She was sitting on the roof patio above the dining room, which faced Mace.

She kissed him hard, but with care.

"I saw your father this morning," he said.

"That must have been historical," she said.

"It was at gunpoint."

She did not pursue it. She handed him a file.

"Read it," she said. "Then let's talk. I'm responsible for everything there. Responsible, guilty, at fault, the instigator, any way you decide."

She left him there to read—alone.

Before she was out of the room he'd scanned the opening page. It was the personal ad she'd put in the necessary newspapers. She got a momentary look at him. His eyes, she thought, looked like they were staring into that dark night of the soul.

Bill left the house and they didn't know it. He had taken to the outside stairwell that went down from the patio to the side garden.

They'd given him about an hour and when he didn't come down Viola went up to check on him. All she found was the file on the table and the patio door open. She saw he'd done a lot of smoking as the ashtray was weighed down with Kools.

The truth or falsity of what this Beonca Costa had written was anyone's guess—but not his.

Alright—Costa had ended up partnering with this Arthur Nussbaum—if that was his name. She went to work with him luring people in bars to private parties, sponsored by a client. At these parties people would be drugged.

What happened to these people she had no idea, and if Nussbaum did, he kept it to himself.

CHAPTER 115

And the whole story about the day of the murder cut the heart right out of him. This Costa woman getting a call from a completely unbalanced Nussbaum, begging for her to come at once to an apartment on Holland and Antin Place, that he would be waiting, hiding on the roof. And when she got there, she was to wait in the car, keep it running and speak to no one, address no one.

She sat in the car, sweating, petrified, and when the shotgun door swung open she could have vomited as he had blood spatters all across his shirt and sport coat.

"Go... go!" He put his foot to the gas.

"Let me get it in gear!" she said.

He was holding the sides of his head, ranting, crying.

"They've drugged me," he said. "The fuckers drugged me."

As she sped away he hid his face in his hands.

"I think I might have killed somebody... on the subway."

BURN EVERYTHING WE'VE GOT… THEN FORGET IT

CHAPTER 116

After Viola went looking for Bill, she discovered his car was gone.

She had no idea he'd driven to the address this Costa woman had written about—Antin Place and Holland Avenue.

There was something about that address.

It was a mile or so away from Pelham Parkway and when Bill got there he realized—he might have been there before.

Holland and Antin formed a V and the apartment on the corner was designed as a triangle. Much like the Flatiron Building in Manhattan. It was seven stories and on the roof was what looked like a water tower from the old days. But it had been reboarded up now and painted and now resembled the tower of a castle.

The real question—he was trying to remember what year it had been. Had his mother been alive, or was she already murdered. It made a world of difference.

The night he'd been to the building he was with Warsh. It was just one night in the life of a boy. Warsh was on an errand. An "errand of mercy," he said, as he set a full garbage bag down on the back seat, making sure it was closed up. What it was filled with sounded like clinky metal.

Warsh stopped at their gas station. He had Bill fill up the tank while he went to the office. This gave the kid enough stolen time to check out what this "errand of mercy" was all about.

The garbage bag had an assortment of handguns.

Bill quickly got back and away and went to watching the gas pump, playing the innocent.

He wanted to ask Warsh that night as they drove to wherever they were going, about the weapons—but he thought better of it, because he was afraid.

All those years later here was Bill pulling up to the street corner. There was the triangular seven story apartment. And there was the painted tower on the roof. And there was the apartment building across the street where Warsh had come with the garbage bag tucked under his arm, leaving the boy to wait in the car while he pressed the entry buzzer to someone's apartment.

Bill walked that patch of Bronx street corner, smoking a Kool, considering how these pieces might fit together.

Where did the lies start, and where did the lies stop. And where will they take you?

He was flicking ash from his menthol cigarette into the gutter, liking to forget the whole thing, not even a pathetic slice of the whole thing, because the thing was you, in you, of you, forever you.

Why did this woman give such detail to the story, or the confession? Bill crossed the street taking the scene in. He had no idea what he'd learn or find or uncover.

Was this just the scene of a con, a lie, a hustler's scam?

Whatever the finality, the Costa woman had a location in her story that matched a place Bill Castle had been to all those years ago.

And the sword of Damocles hanging over Bill Castle's head was his Papi.

CHAPTER 117

While Viola was waiting at Gardner's for Bill to return, if he was going to return, a small crowd of people began to gather in front of the Lourdes Shrine across the street at Saint Lucy's Grotto.

It was the beginnings of a rally, she could see that. Placards, protestors, a banner was being hung up across the top of the shrine—pray for voting rights.

A camera truck pulled up from WPIX. A few reporters were there to cover the scene.

Viola went to her car parked in the driveway and got the camera Malone had given her.

She was taking pictures as part of her internship when someone slid in beside her and said, "I know you."

She turned and there was a young man about her age. Very dark, very Spanish, with a straight up smile, holding a stack of fliers.

"You don't know me," she said, taking one of his fliers.

"Well… I do… sort of. At the college I gave you a flier."

"You didn't give me a flier. There was a girl there who gave me a flier."

She was lying. She had no idea who gave her the flier, but she was gaming him.

"You're right," he said. "I was the charming guy you didn't notice."

"I've noticed you now."

"How would you like to be invited to a rally?"

"Rallies are generally open to the public. That's the idea, right?"

"That's the general idea. Let's change the subject," he said. "My name is Rick."

"Viola."

"Are you part of the revolution?" He jerked a thumb toward the crowd and the camera. "Or are you *goin' round and takin' names*?"

"Ohhh," said Viola. "I know that song."

"I wanted to see if you knew."

"And I know what it means."

"Glad of that too."

CHAPTER 118

While they were talking Viola saw Bill's car pull into the driveway.

"We're gonna have to continue this lively conversation another time," said Viola.

As she started away Rick wrote his name and number down on a flier and pressed it into her hand.

"In case you want to talk politics."

She nodded but was somewhere else.

She caught up with Bill on the front porch.

He looked like one very thought out character. Very conflicted.

"If you're mad at me for what I did... let me have it. I know I opened you up to possible heartache and pain. But I thought—"

He put a hand on her shoulder to quietly silence her. He touched her cheek almost wistfully.

He didn't want to tell her that if this "investigation" was going to be played out, it was going to be at least as terrible for her as for him.

Maybe worse.

Something, a feeling, told him, it would be worse.

CHAPTER 119

When the three had gathered in Gardner's office and he'd told his secretary he didn't want to be disturbed, Bill laid out the truth as he saw it. Short of details, of course.

"Burn everything we've got… and then forget it," said Bill.

"That sets the stage," said Viola, totally upturned.

"I think so," said Bill.

"What… why?"

"Forget why," said Bill. "*Why* can get you in over your head sometimes."

"And the Costa woman?" said Viola.

"Burn her too, if we can get away with it."

Gardner questioned Bill. "How did you come to this decision… assumption?"

"I read the writing on the wall."

Bill started to light up a Kool. But instead he went over to a small portable bar Gardner kept in his office.

"Can I pour anybody a drink?" said Bill.

No takers.

"Alright," he said.

He poured one for himself. Rum and Coke—God bless him. Now he lit that Kool. He went and sat on one of those expensive Gardner antique chairs in the corner of the office. Bill was leaning forward. He took a drink, he took a draw on his cigarette. He looked like a cross between an ill dressed prince and a street tough. He was also swept up in a thought.

"Do you think she's lying?" said Viola.

Bill didn't answer. And not because he couldn't.

"Bill... Do you think Costa is—"

"I think she's capable. I should say I hope she's capable."

"What does that mean?"

"You never know when you're in need of a good liar," said Bill.

"I don't understand," said Viola. She looked to Gardner. "Do you?"

"Do you think Costa is pulling a con job for the money she's demanding?" said Gardner.

"Not likely."

"You mean she's telling the truth?"

"Lying would be better," said Bill.

CHAPTER 120

"Where we go from here," said Gardner, "is the first order of business."

"You got my take," said Bill.

"Where did you go when you left here?" said Gardner.

"For a ride. I took a little trip down memory lane."

"What did you discover?" said Viola.

"It's dripping with memories."

"Was I wrong in doing this?" said Viola.

"The truth is... whatever you did or didn't do was gonna be wrong. Even when you're right. Especially when you're right. And it wasn't your fault being right."

"You're keeping something from us," said Gardner.

"If I am, would I tell you I am?" said Bill.

Viola was pacing. Viola was smoking. Viola was mad because she was hurt, because she felt guilty, because she'd opened the door to forces she did not understand.

"We're in need of an answer," said Gardner. "Costa's information is good or it isn't. Do you meet with her tomorrow or not?"

Bill kept sitting there deep down in his thoughts.

"Say something," said Viola.

"I'm trying to think how this… *bitch*… is trying to sell us information of a crime she's gonna drop on someone… Who may or may not be guilty… And who may or may not be alive." Bill got up.

"We'll meet here," he said. "She's a nightmare. You know that, right?"

"Cause she's a con artist?" said Viola.

"Cause she maybe, maybe, gets us within an inch of the truth."

He took a moment. "Remember," he repeated what the woman dropped on them, "I'm not deaf… I was just being cautious…."

CHAPTER 121

They left together. They stood in the dusky driveway. The rally across the street was in full form. Youth making speeches. Youth with music. Youth with passion. They were not only talking equality through the Voting Rights Act, they were talking equity. The means of closing gaps. They were talking fairness and justice. The rally was a first rate introduction into a stream of ethical consciousness.

"How are you when things go bad?" he said.

"Ask me when they go bad."

"Papi and your father were supposed to go upstate."

"Yeah," said Viola. "Lake George, I think."

"Did they leave?"

"Yeah."

"Anybody at the house? Maid, housekeeper?"

"No maid, no housekeeper."

"You have a gun?"

"A gun... me?"

"In the house... a gun?"

"My father has."

"You know where they are?"

"The guns? ... In the garage... in a latchbox in the floor."

"Find yourself an alibi for tonight," said Bill. "Just in case."

"Whoa," she said. "Just in case of what?"

"The alibi shouldn't be Gardner." Bill pointed to the rally across the street. It had spread out now, taking up most of the grotto and outdoor gardens with its religious statuary.

"You got that internship from Malone, right? For school?"

"Yeah."

"Fix yourself with them. Stay with them."

"When will I see you?"

"I don't know. Your father keep money in the house?"

"He's got one of those TV wall safes tucked behind some blando picture of me in his office."

He started away. No kiss. No nothing. She corralled him.

"You gonna explain all this to me. Including the attitude."

"I don't know. Probably not."

"That doesn't sound too good for our future."

"I hope we haven't sped past our future."

As he walked away now, she shouted after him. "What am I witnessing here?"

CHAPTER 122

Lake George is about two hundred miles north of New York City. It is a resort town in the heart of the Adirondacks on the road to Montreal. It is motels and gift shops, beach fronts and boating. It is the summer on a lake that you carry with you always.

It also had a Howard Johnson's. And who can forget Howard Johnson's?

That's where Charlie Dash and Warsh were to meet Avalon.

"I hate these upstate resort towns," said Charlie, "with their third rate fort restorations… William Henry… Ticonderoga… and phony paddlewheelers cruising the lake."

"The kids love it," said Warsh.

"Frontier Town… Story Town… Santa Claus Village… all dreck."

"You're dripping with cynicism, partner."

"The whole joint is gift shops and eating joints," said Charlie.

"The kids love it," said Warsh.

Charlie had some choice words for Warsh but someone tapped on the window facing their booth before he got the chance to vent.

It was Frankie Avalon. Or a reasonable facsimile.

Avalon entered the restaurant and slid into the booth seat.

"Lot of years," said Avalon.

"You still look like Frankie Avalon," said Charlie. "You don't fuckin' age. How do you pull that off?"

"I drink the blood of my vanquished enemies."

He meant it to be funny. He flagged the waitress and ordered coffee.

"So," said Warsh. "Nat Blue. Talk to us."

"He's alive," said Avalon. "And he's not supposed to be."

"Now you have to ask," said Charlie. "Is he still experimenting with Lucy for somebody?"

"LSD was always his thing," said Warsh. "If he's still working it... if it ever got out what was going down up there on Bedford."

"We're not dealing with that," said Charlie.

"I want you to know," said Avalon, "I would handle this on my own. But my family is here. The kids. And Malone thought, before this guy skips, he'd bring you in. He didn't want the chance of any prints being left around."

"Mr. Blue is getting help somewhere," said Warsh. "Has to be."

"Let's finish up," said Avalon, "and I'll educate you."

CHAPTER 123

There was a string of rental cabins that went from Lake Shore Drive down to the beach. Avalon and his family were in one of those cabins. Just beyond was a row of trees and then the Blue Lagoon Motel, which was very much its own string of cabins down to the beach.

Avalon was taking in the sun when who does he see through that row of trees?

Avalon pointed out the Blue Lagoon cabin where Nat was staying, or hiding out. However you want to describe it.

Except for one night, one hour. There was a man and a woman there, and then gone. A couple he did not recognize, or could name.

"Got any information on how long he's been here for?" said Warsh.

"Those cabins rent by the week," said Avalon. "It's been about that long since I first saw him. He doesn't seem grooved in the place.

And who those two people are and will they be back is anyone's guess."

"Alright," said Charlie. "We go on the basis this has to happen and happen fast."

"Do we take him alive?" said Warsh. "See what we can get out of him?"

"Risky," said Avalon.

"Do we make it look like suicide or an accident?"

No one had a solid answer for that.

"If it goes bad," Charlie said to Avalon, "you think you and your family should have been checked out of your place?"

"No," said Avalon. "I'm a third set of eyes. And I can follow him while you plan. He doesn't have a car."

They started to talk over possibilities, scenarios. Everything was leaning toward shoot him dead and be done with it.

But the law of unintended consequences was hard at work.

CHAPTER 124

Nat Blue usually had a smoke down by the water around dusk. Then he'd take a walk along Lake Shore Drive. Find himself a joint where he could have dinner, nurse a drink, then return to his cabin.

He was pensive, that's how Avalon described him. Always looking as if nervously expecting someone or something. Like the Grim Reaper would maybe come rolling up his ass.

Warsh and Charlie scoped out the cabin. Getting in, the layout, how to leave after the shooting.

Charlie had a silencer. They felt it would be easy putting down their target and getting on with it.

CHAPTER 125

They slipped into the cabin just after dark. While Charlie kept watch Warsh searched the room, the carryalls, anything that might give a hint to the life their target was living.

Warsh whispered, "He's totally spartan."

They'd planned on making the killing look like a robbery, so Warsh tossed the room. Then they waited.

There were voices along the walkway by the cabin that came and went. Lots of memories there for Warsh.

Kids laughing, kids shouting, kids scooting to who knows where. Parents reprimanding them, parents pleading from exhaustion, trying to talk to their kids over transistor radios.

A bygone world Warsh had lived once with Bill and his mother. He'd give it all up to get that back. No chance.

The voices outside thinned out over time. Soon a couple passing veered off the walkway and approached the cabin.

A man and a woman talking quietly—dear God—were now outside the cabin. Warsh could smell the woman's fuckin' perfume.

She knocked on the cabin door. When she and the man with her got no answer they knocked again.

"Nat... you in there?"

Charlie and Warsh could not see each other through the streaked dark, but they knew.

The voices outside whispered even more now, as if talking in secret.

"You think he took it on the road?" said the man.

"I don't know, Artie."

"I guess we wait," he said.

CHAPTER 126

So they did the wait. Charlie and Warsh softly walked the room so they could talk together.

They overheard the woman outside say, "I'm going down to the water and have a smoke."

"I'll come with you," said the man called Artie.

"I don't want company," said the woman.

The man outside was alone now. They could hear his shoes scuffing gravel outside the cabin. They once saw his outline try to see in the window.

"Fuck me," he said.

Charlie and Warsh went through how they'd deal with this new scenario. They were calm and cool, like they had been the time before this, and the time before that.

"It's the woman," said Warsh. "Being down there by the water."

"Hopefully," said Charlie, "she's no fucking sprinter."

LIFE MOVES

CHAPTER 127

When it happens, it's like a car accident. Everything is calm and unassuming, and then it's not.

Eventually Nat Blue showed up. He wasn't so happy to find Artie lingering by the cabin door. Blue had just gotten out the words, "What are you doing—"

The cabin door swung open.

Charlie stepped into the night. Warsh sprinted past Charlie just as he shot Nat Blue right in the head. Nat shit right where he hit the ground. Warsh was sprinting toward the water, scanning the night, trying to spot the woman as he ran.

Artie had enough time to try to escape. A second shot clipped him in the back of the neck, but it did not kill him. He collapsed and went funneling into the lawn. He got out a scream.

Warsh could not find the woman. But there were a couple of teenagers in a float out on the moonlight. The scream drew their attention. Charlie had leaned over and pressed his pistol hard against Artie's skull and fired. That let loose a nasty spray of blood.

Then he took off toward Lake Shore Drive, pocketing his weapon, walking calmly to where Avalon was to be waiting in his car.

Warsh was down by the water. No sign of the woman. But he saw someone was heading toward the open cabin door. That same someone had just started to yell for help. Warsh knew he was out of time. He pocketed his weapon and headed up the far side of the Blue Lagoon Motel toward Lake Shore Drive.

He spotted Avalon's car. Charlie shoved open the car door. As Warsh got in, Charlie said, "You didn't get her."

"I couldn't even find her."

CHAPTER 128

Bill took his motorcycle and drove to Riverdale. He parked a half dozen blocks from the Dash house by the Henry Hudson Parkway. He walked the last of the way up 247th Street to Independence.

It never ceased to amaze him how toney the neighborhood was, and just blocks from the Henry Hudson. At night particularly, as there were no cars parked on the street, and no sidewalks to speak of. Everything was landscaped and beautifully manicured. At night the whole damn place smelled of trees, of being out in the country.

Whenever he saw that rare set of headlights he slipped into the trees in case it was the police. This was not a question answering night. Especially for a lone youth shouldering a satchel who couldn't explain what he was doing there.

Getting into the house was about as easy as it was for his Papi and Charlie Dash slipping into that Lake George cabin.

This was a search and mayhem night.

First came the garage and the lockboxes built into the floor for the guns.

Next was the wall safe. This was about an hour's worth of tricky drilling. The right tools were a must, which he had. But it was his tour of duty in the Spofford reformatory learning the trade that made all the difference.

Next came Dash's office.

CHAPTER 129

At Gardner's office at the appointed hour the following day, Beonca Costa did not appear.

When she was late by half an hour they dealt with it. But as the day wore on, no, no, no, this was not cool.

She did not call. She did not send a message. Nothing.

Viola stood over an extension staring down at it with such rage. She went to throw it across the room. Thought better of it. Gardner got up, took the phone, and he threw it at the wall.

"Does that make you feel better?" he said.

"She ran out on us," said Viola.

"I don't think so," said Gardner.

"I failed," said Viola. She turned to Bill, who was sitting quietly alone, looking out the window toward Saint Lucy's. "I'm sorry," she said.

"You could not have failed," he told her, "what was failed to begin with."

A phone rang.

Was it her?

Gardner's secretary answered the phone.

She got Gardner on the extension.

"Take a message," he said.

And then, "It was not her."

CHAPTER 130

The silence afterward held them captive.

Bill lit up a Kool.

No one had anything to say until Bill came out with "America is closing in."

"What?"

"America is closing in. The corporate nation, man. It's going outlaw and it's hunting down its children."

Gardner had no idea where this was coming from, though Viola did.

"Explain this," said Gardner.

"I can't piece it all together, but I can see some of the pieces. And I can feel some of the others. And there's others yet I'm not sure of and I won't tell you till I know."

He got up. He started out. "No sense in waiting."

Viola swung in behind Bill on the way out the door and stopped him there on the porch.

"This have anything to do with last night?"

He knew she meant his going to her house.

"No… but last night has something to do with this."

He was down the stairs when Viola said, "Are we going home together?"

He stopped in the driveway. "It's all a murky business," he said.

"I don't get it."

"I'm afraid for us."

"We're tough enough… aren't we?"

"We're gonna get swallowed."

"Swallowed? By who? My father? Warsh?"

"By the whole deal."

"How do you know this?"

"There's no other way."

"You gonna go this alone?"

"They say you shouldn't burn your bridges behind you."

"Yeah?"

"I say burn them. Don't give the hunters a chance to catch up."

"I didn't just give you my body... I gave you the rest. Remember that."

CHAPTER 131

They didn't realize that Gardner was watching them from his law library window. He could not hear the words, but he could do his best to interpret their conversation, starting there in the driveway, then crossing the street to Saint Lucy's Grotto.

Viola had a hand in Bill's back pocket. They seemed to Gardner one being really. Connected in the most amorphous of ways and then they stopped and stood in the shadow of the shrine. They were deep in talk, ceaselessly pulling together then pushing away.

This was a talk it seemed to Gardner about decisions, decisions put upon by each other, by the world. Children of the deeds that came before them is what they were, and parents of those decisions that come next.

It would be easier if they were not in love with each other. Gardner knew you cannot traffic in love, as too much pain and drama go hand in hand.

He saw it when she tugged mercilessly at his arm, grasping his short sleeve. He was trying to pull away, but to Gardner it seemed he was not pulling hard enough.

Who was commanding here?

This kind of show of affection leads to suffering. That was the finality Gardner felt in that scene, the way Viola now was shaking her head. Was he turning away to be done with it, was he just overwhelmed by the passion of her passion?

It was not a series of moods he was watching. It was one connected stream of consciousness built around the murder of one of their mothers.

But Gardner also knew all too well the short stories of the people that connected them and that there were secrets yet to go.

He was also a bearer in that burden. A lawyer is like a priest in that way. You carry around people's secrets. Secrets that cannot be shed. And secrets that are not merciful.

They may break up, they may come apart, they may be shattered into a thousand pieces for trying to do the right thing.

But would they be held captive by each other for the same reasons? Gardner could see that as Bill held Viola's face, as he pressed his forehead against hers, and how she clung to him, then let him go only to cling to him again.

They are fighting for the last seconds before their decision takes hold. And how even when they walk away from each other, they will be together.

CHAPTER 132

Viola pulled into the driveway. The front door to her father's house was wide open. She entered the house to find it appropriately ransacked. Like she knew it would be.

Her father appeared at the far end of the entry.

"What happened?" she said.

"Come with me," he demanded.

And she did.

In the garage he pointed to the lockboxes in the floor, drilled open.

"Did you call the police?" she said.

He stared at her as if she should well know the answer.

"Come with me," he said.

And she did.

The painting that covered the wall safe was on the floor. The safe had been drilled open.

"Your boyfriend's handiwork."

"I don't understand."

"Were you with him when he did this, or did you just help set it up?"

"Neither."

"Tell your boyfriend he's starting a war he can't finish."

"He's not my boyfriend anymore."

She looked in the open safe.

"Thank God for that," said her father. "Though it feels like a lie."

There was money in the safe which she took out, held out, showed her father by flashing it.

"Yeah, it's not the money he wanted. He's just letting me know I'm vulnerable."

She put the money back.

"I'm not stupid enough to leave anything compromising in a safe, in my house."

"Why didn't you just go to the police if you know it's him?"

"Because the police want answers... And I deal in everything but—"

"I'm going to take a shower," said Viola, "and try to get clean of all this."

CHAPTER 133

When Bill pulled into the driveway Warsh leaned out the window and yelled for Bill to come on up.

Warsh was in the kitchen, taking two beers from the fridge when Bill walked in.

"Hey there," said Bill.

"Looking good… how do you feel?"

"I don't know yet."

"Wise answer."

Warsh handed Bill a beer. Pointed at the kitchen table for the kid to sit.

"Question," said Warsh. "Have I always shown that I trust you… Have faith in you?"

"Pretty much, yeah."

"Never went down to your place to snoop. To see if you were leading some secret life."

"Not that I know of… though it is an interesting take on present circumstances."

"Yeah… interesting take on present circumstances."

Warsh held out the bottle so they could toast. "Through all the good times and the bad."

And toast they did. Then Bill set the bottle down. He took a pack of matches lying on the table. Lit up a Kool. He looked the matchbook over as he did this, then he tossed it aside.

"I got a call earlier," said Warsh. "And I bet you can guess who from."

"Nope," said Bill.

"You're gonna make me walk the walk."

"I'm not gonna make you do anything, Papi."

Bill picked up the matchbook. Looked it over. Turned it over and over like someone would a coin.

"I heard you and Viola broke up."

"Rumor has it."

"I'm sorry."

"No you're not."

"Well... yes and no."

"Betting odds on no."

"When no is better than yes."

"That is also an interesting take on present circumstances."

Bill swigged down his beer, then he got up and took that short adventure to the fridge for another.

"How was your trip?"

"We've had better," said Warsh.

"Lake George still... Lake George?"

"How did you know we went to—"

Bill reached for the matchbook on the table and tossed it to Warsh. It was one of those advertising matchbooks from some motel on Lake Shore Drive—the Blue Lagoon.

Warsh should have tossed them.

"We got to deal with the Charlie issue," said Warsh.

CHAPTER 134

"Antin Place," said Bill.

"What?"

"Antin Place... Holland Avenue."

Warsh shrugged.

Bill swung the fridge door shut, opened another beer.

"I happened to drive by there the other day and I suddenly flashed on being there once with you. This was way back. You had to drive over there and do some errand.

"You brought along a brown garbage bag. You know, those paper bags you get at the supermarket. You put it in the back seat. It made this funky clanky noise.

"You took me along. It was at night. I don't remember if it was before or after Mom was murdered. Remember now?"

"I don't."

"You stopped at our gas station and went into the office and when you did I snuck a look in the bag."

"Okay."

"There were three, maybe four handguns in the bag."

Calmly Warsh said, "I don't remember that. But anything is possible."

"Antin Place and Holland Avenue. You parked and took the bag and rang a buzzer to an apartment in the building on Holland. Any clearer?"

"No."

"Well… there you go."

"Maybe you're confusing it with a dream, Bill."

"I'm not big on dreams like that."

"I sense discord."

"But it could be true… what I'm telling you."

"This is more and more beginning to feel like an interrogation."

CHAPTER 135

Bill leaned back against the kitchen counter where he could look down on Papi.

"You ever think about how maybe we didn't do enough to find out what happened on the elevated back in the day."

That question hit him.

"That's not a question," Warsh said, "that's a life... None of which I can answer except to say *There would never be enough time.*

"Now... one question for you, kid... Need a cold hard answer. Why is this happening all of a sudden?"

"It takes a long time building to *all of a sudden?*"

"We're living on the dark side of the block now."

"Substantively... yeah."

Warsh was going to ask if this had anything to do with Antin Place and Holland. But that was a full throttle flame he wanted to stay away from.

"You making a life move, Bill?"

"I'm making a life move."

Warsh got up now. Took another beer from the fridge. Then thought—forget it. He went for a bottle of rum he kept in the freezer. He drank from the bottle. "Fuck a glass," he said.

"Yeah," said Bill. "Fuck a glass."

CHAPTER 136

Warsh and Charlie were ordered to Malone's office on Bedford Street in Greenwich Village. Malone had people in Lake George feeding him updates on the investigation into the shooting and murder of two men.

First reports were it was a robbery, but the men were discovered to have their wallets and cash on hand. First reports also said there were probably two shooters, as there were different shell casings at the scene.

There were no reliable witnesses—so far. At best just the usual vague sighting, inconclusive, unsubstantiated.

Not made public were the identities of the two men. One was a former chemical engineer with the army named Nathaniel Blue. The other, who would be identified by fingerprints, was a former military officer who had been dishonorably discharged back in '56. His name—Artie Baum.

"Anything on the woman?" said Warsh.

"You mean the one you let get away."

Warsh remained mute.

"She seems to have escaped the scene completely," said Malone. "But why hasn't she gone to the police?"

"Why were the three together at all?" said Charlie. "After all these years."

There was little more to be said—at the moment—that would deliver.

Nathaniel Blue had been a cutting edge chemist in what would become the nascent COINTELPRO, whose drug experiments, especially the Lucy project, would be used to try to neutralize groups the government decided were subversive. Blue had gone off the deep end, disappeared, and now resurfaced.

CHAPTER 137

Charlie and Warsh had driven there in their own cars. When Malone had a private moment with Charlie he asked him to come back—alone.

Warsh had no idea.

Malone took Charlie to Chumley's Pub so their meeting would look unofficial.

They sat at a quiet table, they had a quiet drink, and then a quiet lunch.

Charlie Dash didn't usually get stressed out in these situations, but today he could feel his own heartbeat.

"I don't like having spirited arguments with myself on certain subjects," said Malone.

Yeah… This was going to be worse than Charlie thought.

"Lake George… losing that woman… letting that woman get away… A woman, for Christ's sake."

Charlie was going to come to his friend's aid, but then he thought better of it.

"I'm losing faith in him," said Malone. And losing faith in a person means you don't have a future with that person."

He sipped his scotch. Malone was always on the right side of being proper, being orderly, officious. He made these feel like terrible human traits one should fear.

"Some men just lose their abilities along the way. The edge… gone. And when they lose it, they have to be dealt with. And this is something you may have to play a vital role in, Charles."

Malone took another sip of scotch.

"Don't lose the edge, Charlie… the world is unforgiving."

CHAPTER 138

Bill was in the gas station garage going about the unenviable and forever tasks of changing spark plugs. This time on a '60 Caddy, when Warsh walked in, just back from his meeting with Malone.

"You don't look good," said Bill.

"No?"

"Well, I should just say you don't look right."

Warsh shrugged the comment off.

"It's just that expression on someone's face that gave me cause for concern."

"I'll take over here, son… Nothing like spark plugs to soothe the savage beast."

"I guess I'll go and get high paying bills," said Bill.

Warsh smiled—sort of. Bill had a transistor on, tuned into WABC doing the top twenty countdown.

Before Bill walked out Warsh said, "When I hear songs back from the day… My day… Your mother's day… When we were teenagers… I can't tell you how desperate I am to be there. To trap the moment. It never goes away. It may sound ordinary, but it offers the truth."

Warsh stared into the grimy Caddy engine. "A guy who doesn't take care of his car… I did what I could, Bill."

"Forget it," said Bill. "Who am I anyway?"

Bill started out.

"The work we do with Malone… You may not believe this, but I think it's important work. And so do the people I work with. Okay… we're on the dark side of the street sometimes… But the country is on the dark side of the street these days.

"America is changing. The people are changing and it's because corruption has got the upper hand. It's got the cutting edge on its side. And that cutting edge is working hard, and it's working better... Yeah, we're on the outside of the law sometimes. What of it? History will judge us. I say we're dedicated heroes. A type of hero, anyway."

"Unsung," said Bill.

"I know how you meant that."

"Do you?"

"What's the real story?" said Warsh suddenly.

"Real story?"

"Holland Avenue and Antin Place."

"It's just what I said."

"You go down a street and flash on a maybe moment."

"Not maybe."

"If you're making a life move, finesse your lies."

Warsh was coming around the Caddy when Bill cut him off.

"What are you bringing this up for? What lie are you carrying around?"

CHAPTER 139

Teatro Puerto Rico was a famous music hall and movie theatre in the Mott Haven district of the Bronx. In a Spanish district, the Teatro built its reputation on Puerto Rican and Spanish entertainers and movie stars like Cesar Romero and Ricardo Montalban.

But this night the theatre was the organizational base camp for the upcoming rally down 5th Avenue for the Voting Rights Act that, up to this point, was still not approved by the city. A rally threatening to happen whether the city permitted it or not.

Viola was looking for where the committee heads of the rally were and was guided around the corner of 138th Street to a former two story store that was now a church. The window had a beautiful, full size, hand painted Christ and beneath the crucifix it read: *Iglesia Christiana – Juan 3:16.*

The upstairs, which at one time had been huge storage rooms, was now a meeting hall that was packed to overflowing.

A young woman with an army shirt draped in spangles and passion to boot stood in front of a full size map of 5th Avenue and spoke to the room.

"Those of you," said the woman, "who signed up to be squad leaders in the rally will most likely be the first to be arrested, as the police will be looking for the ringleaders.

"There will also be police working undercover. There's probably one or two of them in here right now."

This got a rousing hand of applause as the woman cupped her hands over her eyes like she was an Indian scanning the crowd.

"And yes, there will be people working the rally who've been paid to fake being one of us. Who mean to take down voting rights… and what it stands for. Who are probably racist and bigoted but their business is causing violence. They want to keep us down… Black… Spanish… Puerto Rican… People of Color."

She held up her black arm. This got applause.

"Even whites," she said. "They want us to seem like we are embracing fascism and warthink so they can brand the movement as anti-American."

There were no seats so Viola was standing with her back against the wall.

"Hey, you...."

It was Rick again, leaning over Viola's shoulder.

"You're everywhere," she said.

"As are you," said Rick.

"It's like pure magic," said Viola, with a little cut to her voice.

"Do you think you could be a squad leader?" he said.

"Do you think you could?"

"I have been," he said. "A couple of times."

"I'll be breaking my cherry, then," she said. "But I've broken a cherry before."

This tripped him up some.

"Your boyfriend here?"

"What boyfriend?" she said.

"The guy I saw you run off with at Saint Lucy's Grotto."

"Oh, him."

She didn't like this line of questioning.

"He's not my boyfriend... anymore. Or at least that I know of."

"Was it politics or unfaithfulness?"

She didn't answer that. She lit a cigarette in lieu of it.

"Don't you want someone who thinks like you? Has the same politics... Beliefs?"

"Then one of us would be useless... yes? I know where you're going," she said.

"You've been there," he said.

"I can still see my dust settling."

DESERT BOOTS

CHAPTER 140

It was about three in the morning when a cab pulled up to Gardner's house and he got out, appropriately wasted. And he wasn't alone. Trucking along beside him, and just as stoned, was a character straight out of the Marlon Brando playbook.

The two men had to hold each other to keep upright and Gardner unlocked the front door and they entered in the dark and Gardner made his fumbling way to his office to see if there were any messages left for him.

"Even wasted, you're working," said Brando Junior.

Gardner felt around for the light and flipped it on and he jerked back as a burst of fear came out of the guy with him.

There was a shadow person sitting in Gardner's chair and a shadow gun lay on the desk before him.

It was Beonca Costa.

The guy who'd been with Gardner was gone. He'd seen the person, he'd seen the gun, he'd seen enough.

"You killed this night," said Gardner.

"Sorry."

"How'd you get in?"

"It's one of my skills. I needed a safe place. So…."

"What's going on? Why are you here like this? And the gun?"

She was still wearing that black and white VOTING RIGHTS T-shirt for the Rainbow Rally.

"What's going on with that?" he said, pointing at the shirt.

"It's about getting away clean from the dudes that were after me."

"What do you mean? And why the gun?"

She took a cigarette of hers from a pack on the desk beside an ashtray. Gardner saw she had gone through quite a few in her wait.

"I'm here because there's been a murder." She held her pack of cigarettes out. "Care for one?"

CHAPTER 141

Gardner called Bill at home, then he called Viola who had returned from the Teatro. He did not confide to either the other had been contacted and was coming. He did admit Beonca Costa had a story to tell, and urgency was required. He wanted her to tell it fresh, under his questioning.

When Viola arrived and Gardner opened the front door, who was right there in the hallway entrance—Bill.

Viola gave Gardner a kill shot look.

"Yeah," he said. "I thought it best this way."

Beonca was in Gardner's office, in a chair, having a drink and still wearing that black and white VOTING RIGHTS T-shirt.

When Viola and Bill had a moment to get a word with each other, she said, "How are you?"

"Rotten," he said. "How are you?"

"Rotten," she said.

"Good," he fired back.

Costa stood up. She had stripped off the T-shirt and tossed it to Viola. "I'm not big on the fuckin' revolution... I'm here for revenge."

She looked at Viola and Bill. Said nothing. She waited on Gardner.

"This is about a murder," he said.

"Two murders," said Beonca.

"Yes," he said. "Two murders. Committed at Lake George in the last seventy two hours."

"That I was witness to…."

"Yes," said Gardner. "That you were witness to."

"But before we get into that, I want to… there are rules," said Beonca. "I originally wanted money when I came to you. New rules. I will need some money… A thousand dollars.

"Whatever else I need I will get it the old fashioned way. I can make a living as long as they have subways."

CHAPTER 142

Gardner opened a cabinet door in his credenza. Slid out a tape recorder. Set it all up. Had a microphone he placed on his desk, and there he had Beonca sit.

"The rights to this are mine," she said. "Until I turn it over to you all… I will also be protected… with your silence.

"You'll want to sell this someday… after we get it all out. Real money. But you have to keep it until I say go… or if I'm killed."

She set her cigarettes down on the desk, beside an ashtray. "I'd like something to drink here. Anything will do… Please."

Viola went to the kitchen and returned with a glass of wine.

Costa took a few sips. Her mouth was dry.

"Ready?" said Gardner.

"Yes."

"What is the name of the man you were in Lake George with?" said Gardner. "And what is the name of the man you were there to see?"

"Arthur Baum is the man in Lake George I was there with... and had known all the way back into the mid fifties and to the time of Bill's mother's death... murder. He also went by different names... such as Nussbaum.

"As for the man we were there to see... His name was Nathan Blue."

"And why were you in Lake George to see this Nathan Blue? What was your business?"

"We were going to use your personal ad in the papers to extort him."

"And how were you going to lay out this extortion?"

"Lay it out?"

"You have to extort someone over something. What was that something?"

"Nathan Blue worked indirectly for the U.S. government. His job was to pull in people and use them for drug experiments. Unknowingly, of course."

"You did this how?"

"It was put in their food, put in their drinks, coffee, anything and everything. It was injected. Even aerosols."

"These were illegal drugs? Experimental drugs?"

"Yes. Blue was a chemist. And instrumental in the creation of these drugs and the development of these drugs. They were mind control sort of things. Drugs to break down the enemy's brain... That was how they talked it up."

"You were going to expose him. Threaten him anyway."

"Oh yeah... he'd been fired. He'd gone recluse for years."

"How did you three come into contact with the men who tried to kill you?"

"I have no fuckin' idea how they got on to us."

Beonca took another drink of wine.

"I don't know. It's bad news," she said. "It's bad news for me… and it's bad news for you."

She looked around the room.

"Alright," said Gardner. "At this point… let's get to that night in Lake George. The killings at the cabin first… How many men were there hunting you?"

"I don't know if they were hunting us. They could have been after Blue. And we just—"

"Wrong place, wrong time," said Gardner.

"Don't forget the rest," said Beonca.

"Which is?"

"Wrong place, wrong time, wrong life," said Beonca.

Gardner nodded. "How many?"

CHAPTER 143

"Two… I believe. Maybe three. If they had a car waiting somewhere."

"Could you identify them?"

"Only one… and that was by his shoes."

"Clarify," said Gardner.

She smoked. Flicked ashes into an ashtray she had on her lap. She laughed before she spoke. She had a wiry laugh. One that seemed full of contempt.

"You know who the best con men are? Women. Best liars, best frauds, best hustlers. Women also have this high degree of empathy which fucks with people's heads. Men especially. But of all talents to have, you know which has the post position? I'll bet you don't."

This woman, Gardner thought, leaves a lot to be desired. He glanced at Viola.

"Why don't you tell us," he said.

"Luck," she said. "Pure, unadulterated luck."

She then told him how she'd been down at the beach, sitting on the hull of an overturned rowboat that belonged to the motel.

She was just stubbing out her cigarette in the sand when Nat Blue came around the cabin, saw Art at the door waiting, and when he opened the cabin door there was a sudden gunshot flash.

Another gunshot flash followed that and a man screaming out and another man sprinting down to the water in Costa's direction. She assumed that man was after her, or looking for her.

She couldn't run. She was not fast. She just dropped to the ground by the boat and there she saw there was just enough space between the side of the boat and the sand for her to slink through and hide under the hull.

She explained how the fool, whoever he was, did not think to look under the boat. Maybe he hadn't seen her at all. But she could see his shoes. He was standing two feet away in the dark.

They were desert boots, she explained. Chukka boots, crepe soled. Great boots, cool, but not fit for rain.

He was there a few moments, then he was gone.

CHAPTER 144

There were people by then at the cabin, shouting for help. She crawled out from under the boat. The first Costa saw was a ripple of water from the moon. She made her way up through the darkness of the trees, a plain nobody, disinterested. She reached Lake Shore Drive.

It was fast thinking after that. Got to keep the panic in check. That's essential. You try to avoid the jaws of death. Whoever these murderers were, wherever they crashed the party from, you had to keep your game up.

She walked down Lake Shore Drive. It was late, still a nice crowd of tourists roamed about. Did the two men she saw have any idea who she was? Did they know what she looked like? Did they have someone waiting in a car? They wouldn't try to escape the scene on foot. Were they hunting now for her?

She had enough money to catch a Greyhound to Saratoga. Getting out of Lake George was a must. If they knew what she looked like they would work the town. The bus depot would definitely be on their check out list.

She wore a coat which she took off and dumped in the trash. She had a shoulder bag with about half a dozen phony pairs of glasses, so she could change her look when she was plying her trade.

Costa got hold of a bus schedule. She scoped out the depot from the dark, looking over people waiting on the Saratoga Greyhound, trying to find a mark.

And what does she see? Three youths in their twenties, part of the hipster crowd. Pot and sex and social justice. All of them wearing the same T-shirt that had printed on it: *VOTING RIGHTS—Equality comes in every color. Join the Rainbow Rally on 5th Avenue.*

She had on a pair of bookworm glasses and saw where they sat and with a hustler's beauty talked her way into their life stories. She was like a family member in ten fleet minutes flat.

They had a bag filled with T-shirts they were going to sell at the rally and pay for their eats. And Beonca bought one and put it on right then and there.

Finding three marks like this was better than finding religion. And one even had a wallet that was born for being picked.

CHAPTER 145

When she was done, it was not as if all questions had been answered. In truth there were still gaping holes in the facts. And new realities that put unnamed forces in dangerous proximity. There was also something that Bill would bring up later. When the Costa woman was not in the room.

"I know what you're thinking," said Beonca.

"Do you?" said Gardner.

"If the men know me, do they have a plan to find me. Kill me. Can they execute that plan. Are they now at risk, or at least think so. And are we all now at risk? Because of me."

Viola cut in. "We're at risk now because of me... I set this in motion with the personal ad. And for that—"

"You're a bitch after my own heart," said Costa. "Press the advantage, girl."

Beonca finished her wine in a few hard core seconds. She got up and started out. "I'll call you all by payphone. If you got to get to me in an emergency, send a wire to General Delivery... Have it read 'B... it's me.'"

"Where are you going?" said Gardner.

"Hunting," said Beonca.

She reached the door. "Tight and sweet, people," she said. "You can keep the T-shirt. You know, there's one thing I didn't expect. That not a one of us would suggest going to the police. Think about that."

CHAPTER 146

Costa could read the three of them like a book. Decent souls now riding a secret. Smart as they were, and they were smart. She could tell you right now, walking down the street, what each of their impressions were of all they heard. And now the Lake George Murders dropped right into their laps. She was sure they were dissecting the idea that she might be behind them herself.

She headed over to 2200 Esplanade where she could catch the subway down to Manhattan. The Pelham Parkway station was a faceless nothing of a small concrete building on an open stretch of street. The building to her always looked like one of those large mausoleums over at Saint Raymond's Cemetery, where her own father was buried.

Mr. Raphael Costa—thief, con man, and murderer. Who would always tell her in his line of work, and to succeed, it's always best to look like that station building—faceless, nondescript, and especially harmless.

Costa thought the lawyer and the girl were sane and cultured. The young hardcase with those dark fire eyes was another story altogether. He was at heart an outsider. And he carried a gun. She felt it when she slipped past him once in the den. She thought he might carry and she meant to be sure.

This was not a cat who carried it for show. He dealt in the human currency of violence. He had to be watched out for.

On the trip downtown all this made her flash on her father. He'd made her work up her skills on this very train. Maybe even in this very car. Who knows. All the cars were pretty ratted out and old.

CHAPTER 147

Once Costa had gone and it was down to the three, Gardner threw out his arms. "Let the good times flow," he said with some sarcasm.

Viola looked across the room at Bill. "He thinks she's a fraud."

"How do you know that?" said Bill.

"I cruise around inside your head during my free time... even if you don't notice."

"You're a bitch after my own heart," said Bill, stealing a line from the Costa woman.

"Is she right?" said Gardner.

"She's accurate. I don't think she's right. Costa could be a fraud. Look at the Lake George newspapers... the two men dead. What if she was the shooter. Killed them both. What if it was a plan and we're fronts. Not alibis but certainly the next best thing."

"Her story certainly undercuts what she told us originally," said Gardner. "It also kills her chance of getting money from us because we can never prove now this Art Baum was the killer of your mother.

"But the new story tells a different story. Can she exploit us with that? Yes... or no?" said Gardner.

"She's too slick for my tastes," said Viola.

"And all that drama about revenge," said Bill.

"Don't question women working out of revenge," said Viola.

"Do we cut her loose, see what happens? Or do we keep on?" said Gardner.

"She didn't cut us loose," said Viola.

"Why hasn't she?" said Bill.

"It could be she's just a walking scam," said Viola.

"Or she's telling the truth," said Gardner.

This simple reality did not seem so simple, or so real.

"Did you see any fear in her?" said Bill. "Any at all?"

No one had.

"This is a woman claiming someone tried to kill her. She barely escaped. Is she looking over her shoulder in desperation? I don't think so. Or that someone is on her. After her. That she is the one 'hunting.' Did you see any fear at all?"

"No," said Viola.

Neither had Gardner.

"What does that tell you," said Bill.

CHAPTER 148

On the train deep down in the darkness Beonca Costa thought of her life and what story next to tell. Building empathy from people combines the heart of a truth and the soul of a lie. And what better place to work this out than on a subway car. After all, the subway had been her home growing up, it had been her grade school, her library, high school, college. It had been her freedom, it had been her prison.

CHAPTER 149

The money Gardner had given her—fine. The money she could skim from slipping wallets and purses—fine. But she was working for a kill shot. A Lee Harvey Oswald on JFK kill shot that would serve to take down her personal enemies, exploiting everyone to finish her cause.

Does she talk up a mother story to further exploit their empathy? A mother raising her alone, working the subways, with her daughter learning the trade, the craft, under the supervising eyes of a remorseless con woman who was not past beating the girl into misery for any failures.

The trade came first, the craft. The subway car is the bitter refuge like the world itself. Heartless and cold in winter, humid and hellish in summer. No overtime, no job security, no love. Only the endless screech of the wheels, and a stenched out air that grimes your throat like some kind of greasy exhaust choking the truth out of you.

By the time the Costa woman reached Grand Central it was raining. She had rented a storage locker there. In it was a leather carryall and an overnight bag. It was, to put it bluntly, all of her worldly possessions.

She went to the ladies' room and took up in a stall. From the leather carryall she removed a small revolver. She gave it a check, though she knew it was loaded and ready to go. She had an extra box of shells. These, and the weapon, she slipped into her shoulder bag.

She went into the Terminal Bar and took up a seat in a quiet corner. She ordered a drink, she bought a newspaper. The newspaper was just a front to keep away the dregs who might approach with the aim of creeping into her panties.

She sat there silently working things through her mind. She knew the man she was hunting out, and yet she didn't. She knew where he'd been, but not where he was now. She heard his name, but didn't remember it. It had been so long for all of that. She'd slipped through the cracks of time, but she would find him.

She did have one small betting chip in her favor.

CHAPTER 150

"I have to shut down for the night," said Bill.

"Makes sense," said Gardner. "We've gone about as far as we can, for now."

He got up from his desk and started to close down the tape recorder, respooling the tape, then putting it in its storage box. "I'm going to keep it in my safe. Only you will have legal access to it… if something should befall me… shared access… together."

Gardner looked at Viola. She was watching as Bill got his stuff together. It seemed she was waiting for him to say something, something more, something else. Something about them, about now, about what's next… About emotions.

"Do you have to go?" she said suddenly.

Gardner thought she sounded hurt.

Bill was silent, in a conflicted way, it seemed. And to Gardner he looked terribly lonely, tortured, you might say.

"Nothing like washing up on the shores of silence," said Viola.

"You two can camp upstairs, if you like. Go to it."

"Let's go upstairs," said Viola. "For a while, at least."

"You want to talk it out," said Gardner. "I'm going to crash… Am I making myself clear… Yes… No… I wouldn't answer me either."

He started for upstairs, killing all the lights along the way, intentionally leaving Bill and Viola in the dark.

"I vote we stay here in the dark," said Viola. "Talk to each other like strangers. It can be very intimate, talking like strangers. Very cathartic."

He picked up his coat, his cigarettes. Had to feel around for them on the credenza.

"What's the point of running," said Viola. "We're gonna get back to this moment… No matter how many lives we live in between."

He put on his jean jacket, slipped cigarettes and matchbook into its pocket.

"Say something… anything… even if it's a lie… A lie would even be alright. As long as it was interesting."

He opened the door. She pushed her hand against it so it would not open enough for him to get out.

"Please," she said. "Don't disappear into yourself like it's somewhere else, safe."

He forced her hand loose of the door. She let herself be defeated.

"I feel like I've done something terribly wrong," she said.

"You haven't. I can tell you that."

"No?"

"Not even a hint."

"At least that's a start… What next?"

He took a breath and going out the door, said, "I think Warsh might be involved in the Lake George Murders."

CHAPTER 151

He was out the door and on the porch looking into the soft, warm rain. Viola was right on his tail. She neither understood what he said nor could believe what he said.

"Is this some wild thing you locked onto? Some crazy notion?"

"I wish crazy."

"You have any facts to back this up? Was it something that Costa said?"

He took a book of matches from his jean coat pocket and handed it to her.

"I don't understand."

"Look it over. See what's printed there."

The matchbook was from a motel on Lake Shore Drive.

"That motel," said Bill, "is right next to the motel where the two men were shot… Lake George."

He pointed to where it was printed.

"See," he said.

"Where'd you get it? What does it mean?"

"From Warsh. I got it from him. He said he was in Lake George on business. And that was at the same time as the murders."

"Not possible," she said.

"Warsh also had pair of those shitass desert boots Costa talked about," said Bill. "He's got a pair right now in his hall closet. I checked. They're potted with brake fluid, oil, work shop grease… and beach sand."

He held his hand out and started catching drops of rain in his palm. He held his hand out like that and let the rain spill over its edges in long beaded streams.

"Your hand is shaking," she said.

"That's just what I was looking at," he said.

Then something dawned on her.

"My father," she said.

Bill just kept looking at his hand.

"Was my father with him?"

"I wasn't suggesting your father had anything to do with this."

"Translation… that means he was with Warsh."

"Yeah… it means he was with Warsh."

She moved close to Bill now. She could smell the flesh on his neck. His dark hair had a few beads of rain here and there. He looked older, more mature, or at least more edgy. The rain was soothing for a little while. But it didn't last. She looked at the matchbook, then handed it back to him as if it were toxic.

CHAPTER 152

"Why were they in Lake George? Did he tell you?"

"Warsh said it was to deliver money to someone. He didn't name the someone, of course."

"That could be true," said Viola. "Right? It could be true?"

"Yeah," said Bill. "It could be true. They have also told me they were at Lake George to go waterskiing."

"Yeah," said Viola. "I hear you."

"And it just so happened the Costa woman was up there," said Bill. "With this Art Baum. At the same place, at the same time. The two disconnected groups whose stories overlap. What does that tell you... What does it feel like?"

She did not answer because she was temporarily prisoner of this new reality that brought with it an edict of bad news, and then worse news.

"I'm scared," she finally said.

"You can add me to that list."

Then she did something that caught Bill by surprise. She dipped the tips of two fingers in the little pool of rain that was still collecting in his palm. And once she'd done that she blessed him and then herself.

"If you're right," she said. "If this is what is... if what we know right now is right... then what?"

He turned his hand over and let the rain spill away.

"Then we're all we've got."

CHAPTER 153

They had sex with unrestrained desperation in the upstairs apartment of Gardner's house. But no amount of passion, no amount of sweat or raw physicality, would help them escape, no way. No will of mind, no power of soul will save you from having to save yourself. Because the dark truths of a rigged universe are out there waiting, and they both knew it.

Lying in bed with the rain against the window, Bill said, "We should not have done this."

"But we did," she answered.

"It's hard enough to deal with what's happening."

"I wish there was a moon tonight," she said. "A full moon, a clear sky."

"What's wrong with the rain?"

"Nothing, I guess. I just wish it were different. The world around us… I guess. The rain is too intense with reality."

There was a slight ruffle of sheets as she shored up against him.

"How can you be sure?" she said.

"Of what?"

"That it's Warsh."

"I'm only as sure as I was ten minutes ago."

"If Warsh is part of this, then so is my father."

"I suspect so."

"One is your enemy, one is mine," she said.

"Here today, gone tomorrow," he answered.

"Don't say that. Don't speak like that. I can't defend myself against that kind of thought, so I can't defend you."

"Right now," he said, "I wish life moved at the speed of light."

"Because?" she said.

"We'd know by now what happened... What will happen would be behind us."

"If they did this," she said, "what do we do now?"

"If they did this act, and they find out somehow that we found out... What do they do?"

CHAPTER 154

When Viola awoke, Bill was not there. It was still night, but very late. There was only the whoosh of water up through the wheel wells of the occasional car passing on the street below.

She sat up. Looked around in the dark for Bill. Noticed the door to the patio was open.

She got up thinking—he couldn't be out there in the rain. But he was.

He was sitting on one of the wrought iron chairs around the glass patio table, and holding an umbrella. He was also quite naked.

She tiptoed out into the drizzly darkness and came around him and sat under the umbrella on his lap.

"What is this," she said. "You going Mary Poppins on me?"

"I was just thinking," he said, "how our lives are going from inescapable reality to inescapable reality."

"You're either under fire or under water," Viola said. "That's a little aside my father throws at me from time to time... I'm sorry about the ad. And where it's taking us."

"Something else would have come along... Because it's out there. It's alive."

"You think?"

"They do work for the government, right?"

"Right."

"That means their crimes are bigger than they are."

She'd never thought that. But now—

CALIFORNIA SUN

CHAPTER 155

As soon as Bill got home, his phone rang. It was Warsh. "I'm cooking breakfast. You up for it?"

Warsh cooked. Bill fueled up on coffee.

"All nighter?" said Warsh.

Bill lied. Gave out with this tale about picking up some chickie in a Village bar.

Each man was working the other, but neither knew it—yet.

"Seen Viola?"

"Haven't seen Viola."

"Thinking about Viola?"

"Thinking about not thinking about Viola."

Warsh made pancakes. He'd already made bacon and eggs.

"A muscular breakfast," said Warsh.

Bill got up and stole two beers out of the fridge. Handed one to Warsh. "Yes?" Bill said.

"Go reckless," said Warsh, taking the beer.

They sat, they ate, they drank beer.

"The good old days revisited," said Bill.

"Hey... I'm not ready for that good old days thing... Too young yet."

"Don't let it break your heart," said Bill.

"Hey," said Warsh. "What was that song you used to play last year?"

"I played a lot of songs last year."

"About California."

Bill had to think a minute.

"'California Sun'... by the Rivieras," said Bill.

"I don't know who by."

Bill sang a few bars.

Warsh snapped his fingers a bunch, then said, "That's it."

"What are you suddenly... a record aficionado?"

"I heard it a couple of days ago at the station. Those two guys with the fifty seven Plymouth and its rotten muffler. It was on the radio."

"What about it?"

CHAPTER 156

"It got me thinking about you."

"No kidding," said Bill. "About me? I'm honored."

"Don't make a joke."

"I'll be more careful."

"California... You used to talk about it all last year. Part of the American dream... California. You were hot to drive out there and see what it offered."

Warsh took a drink of beer. Wiped his mouth with a napkin.

"I could bankroll you. I would bankroll you. I could set you up for, say, a year. I know some people out in Los Angeles. I did Army time with them.

"See it as an adventure… for right now. Before you get older and life tightens up."

"Has life tightened you up?" said Bill.

"Ask me in ten minutes… or when I finish this beer."

"Do you think life tightens you up? Does you in?"

"Ask me in ten years."

Bill moved the food around a little on his plate. "Do you consider your life a success?"

"How do you mean success? Ethically… morally… righteously… pragmatically…"

"How do you?"

"Not the way you do."

"What do I have to do with how?"

"What you meant is… Would I consider my life a success? Do I rise and fall on your terms… on your expectations?"

"I never thought of it that way… but I guess you're right," said Bill.

Warsh got up to pour more coffee.

CHAPTER 157

"By the way," said Bill, "how was Lake George? Still like that time you, my mother, and I went?"

Warsh stared at Bill over the rim of his coffee cup. Just a pair of eyes and memories.

"Still fake Americana and sunbathing," said Warsh. "Fort William Henry... the paddlewheeler that did day tours... Heaven for ten year olds...."

"And a bane for their parents," said Bill.

"Seriously... the America that never was, comes to life."

"Ever regret not marrying and having a family of your own?"

Warsh's expression spoke of a time passed, a world passed.

"There was your mother... and there's you."

Bill nodded. "Good answer." He finished his breakfast.

Warsh was watching him all the while. It was slipping away... their world.

"Give it some serious thought," said Warsh.

"What?"

"California."

Bill started singing "California Sun" as he took care of the dishes.

"I hope you take me up on the offer," said Warsh.

Warsh was talking code, and the kid didn't need some lingo translator to get it. They were on the tripwire of a flat out warning. And there was not a lot of space between everything that had gone down and what could go down next. Family or not.

CHAPTER 158

Charlie Dash was in his den typing up an itinerary for the priest he and Warsh would be allegedly chaperoning back to Laos, when his daughter peeked in.

"Good morning," she said.

Charlie looked at his watch.

"Yes... I stayed out all night. I just got in. I did not see Bill. How was your trip?"

"Boring," he said.

"Nothing eventful, then?"

"Boring is… boring." Then he added, "Are you completely beyond my control now?"

"Not completely. I am about ninety nine percent beyond it."

"Then I'm hanging by a thread," he said.

She came around his desk and he leaned over and he covered up what he was writing.

"I was not going to snoop."

"Rules," he said.

She kissed him on the cheek. "That's what I was coming around the desk to do."

This softened up his edges.

Then she kissed him again. Said, "I'm sorry."

"What are you sorry for?"

"Think of the kiss as a holding cell for all the *I'm sorrys* for everything I did, might do, could do, possibly do, maybe do that does not meet with your approval."

He noticed now up close the T-shirt she was wearing. The black T-shirt with the rally information that the Costa woman had tossed her.

"Where'd you get that?" he said.

"At the Teatro. They were having a rally meeting."

"The city hasn't approved it yet."

"It doesn't matter. It's been approved by the people."

"So you're one of them now?"

"You better keep watch. You may find the revolution at your doorstep."

"I'll make a note of it."

"It's not just about voting."

"No…?"

"It's about hunting out corruption… moral corruption."

He looked at her squarely.

"That's a left field comment."

"I know. How's it sound coming from me?"

"Threatening… in a quietly hostile kind of way."

"Sounds about right."

She walked around his desk.

"Am I gonna have to watch out for you?" her father said.

"You're supposed to watch out for me… politically speaking I'm your daughter."

She took a framed photograph from the office breakfront. It was Viola with her father. Taken in better days.

"I need to borrow this."

"What for?"

"I want to have a copy made for me."

CHAPTER 159

Viola had lied about the photograph, though she would have to get a copy to serve her purpose.

She packed up a few things, enough for overnight, anyway, and got into her car and drove to Lake George. Once there she got hold of a local map, one of those tourist guides with all the sights, food joints, trinket shops, and motels.

She parked at one end of Lake Shore Drive and then walked it going from motel to motel.

She would enter the office and say "Hello" to whoever was working the desk. Then she would say, "Maybe you could help me?"

She'd then hold out the photograph.

"I know this is a long shot," she would say, "but my family is looking for this man. He's our father. He's an alcoholic and disappears from time to time on these drinking binges. And I was wondering if maybe you'd seen him recently. Maybe he'd even stayed here."

Whoever was behind the desk would listen politely, sympathetically, would take the photograph and study it. They would always give it a long look over, if for no other reason than to be courteous.

"He disappears from time to time. He's a kind man."

"Have you checked with the police?"

"No luck there. My father usually holes up in a motel alone… or with another drinking buddy of his."

Whoever was behind the desk would shake their head despairingly and apologize for not being of any help.

The last motel was a line of cabins just down from Fort William Henry. One of the cabins was where the murders had taken place. Keeping an innocuous distance she walked to the cabin, passed the front door. It was all as Beonca had said.

Then Viola looked down to the beach. It was a short walk. And there was a boat turned over in the sand. Viola wondered if that was the boat Beonca had talked about.

She walked around the boat. She knelt down. There was enough space for someone not too big to squirrel under. The Costa woman could have.

Viola tried to turn the boat over. It was not going well until two teenage boys came by sprinting straight for the shore.

She called to them. Made up a story about how she lost the key to her cabin and they were gonna charge her for it. And could the guys—

She made a flip over motion with her hands. The boys got it. Set the boat over like nothing.

CHAPTER 160

Whatever she was hoping to find, forget it. It was just an empty shell. Like the whole trip.

She got in her car and started home. She'd had nothing to eat, nothing to drink. It was cigarettes all the way.

She stopped at a food stand, ordered a beer and two hard boiled eggs, and hit the road. She got a few bites down, a few swigs down. Then she started to cry.

She cried so hard she should have pulled the car over, but she didn't. She thought maybe it was seeing all those parents and their kids doing the family thing. That high wire walk of joy and chaos.

But the reason was simpler and more sinister. She had come all this way to see if she could learn that her father was involved in two murders, possibly government sanctioned murders.

And the most important aspect, the most honest and direct aspect, the most painful aspect, the aspect that ambushed her heart, was that he was fundamentally capable of such an act, and that even without evidence, she believed him guilty.

CHAPTER 161

Everything the late Art Baum had said to Beonca Costa that day, all those years ago, she carried around like you would a poison pill. And the neighborhood... it looked too much the same even after all those years. And she hated places that looked the same, because that usually meant they were the same.

"If anything should happen to me," Art had said that day, "anything terrible… anything you don't believe… anything that leaves you suspicious that I've been a victim of violence… it will come from this place."

They were double parked, Beonca at the wheel, Art Baum sitting low in the shotgun seat so as not to be seen.

He had been pointing at an apartment on the corner of Commerce and Bedford. This was a toney Manhattan neighborhood. The buildings were three, four, five stories. Most were apartments, brick. Some were homes, some townhouses. There were trees decorously planted along the sidewalk. This was where money and taste came to live. Where people didn't die, they just enjoyed an invisible life forever and ever.

"The parties I'd set up came back to here," Art had said. "The drugs the victims unknowingly took came back to here. People that disappeared came back to here."

The street was still slick from the previous night's rain. It was still gray, and Sunday quiet. The Costa woman walked past the building the recently murdered Art Baum had pointed at.

She looked in the front door window. The building had a small, quiet lobby, with plush carpeting and brass mailboxes and matching elevator door.

CHAPTER 162

She glanced up and down the street. She had already slipped a lock-pick from her shoulder bag. A well practiced turn and a quick, quiet moment later she was in the lobby of 81 Bedford Street.

It could have been a funeral home entry, short of that sickly sweet flower smell. She looked about a bit, then she ran the lock-pick slowly along the names above the mailboxes. Each with its own beautiful brass plate as a small acknowledgment to the tenant's importance.

Catty corner to the apartment was an elegant Italian bakery with half a dozen indoor tables. You had a clear view of the front door of the Bedford apartments and Beonca Costa posted herself at a table where she could inconspicuously watch the comings and goings.

She brought a newspaper the first day, and a textbook after that, to fake reading while she watched and waited for the man Art Baum had pointed out all those years ago.

"He's the devil," Art had said. "And worse than that... he's government."

CHAPTER 163

The priest was packing a bag. He was getting set to be driven to Westchester, where he'd board a private transport destined for Laos. Malone was having a small party in honor of the good work the priest had done.

The priest wanted very much to return to his homeland and continue the fight. But there were many vulnerabilities to that, as he was bearing so much information now about Malone and his operations.

Those in attendance at the party were Charlie Dash, Warsh, and Avalon, who spoke fluent French.

When they left, Charlie was behind the wheel. Warsh sat up front. The priest and Avalon were in the back. The priest was dressed in everyday garb. The priest was not carrying any identification, but reality was, he wouldn't need any.

Malone had come downstairs with the others. The car being parked out front, there Malone said a last goodbye to the priest, shaking his hand.

Beonca knew the moment she saw Malone. He had not changed. He had only grown more chiseled, more set. His thick, blond, straight hair was still thick, blond, and straight. And he still parted it the same way. He still wore the same classy and upscale suits like the classy and upscale suits of years ago.

He could have been years ago. The outlier maintaining a strict compliance with the unyielding rules of the road.

CHAPTER 164

After they pulled away Malone did not go back into the building. But rather he started up the street, then crossed over.

He was heading straight for the bakery.

It was lunch hour, patrons coming and going. Malone ordered a coffee and pastry to go.

Beonca watched him from her table. She did a slight check on where he carried his wallet.

God could not have given her a better opportunity. As Malone headed out there was a woman with a stroller struggling to get in.

He had to wait, give her the right of way. The Costa woman got up and headed for the door, passing within a breath of him.

He did not realize his wallet was missing until he returned to his office.

Beonca took up across the street and waited to see how it would all go down. Within a few minutes he was out the front doors walking quickly, scanning the sidewalk. He returned to the coffee shop. Got hold of the hostess.

Beonca watched an animated conversation. Malone was asking about his wallet. The hostess was nodding. She had him follow her. She went behind the counter. Next thing she had a wallet in her hand. She was telling him about it being found on the floor by a woman. He must have asked where the lady was because the hostess looked around. She was obviously nowhere to be found. Once outside Malone looked through his wallet to see what, if anything, had been taken.

CHAPTER 165

Malone was standing at his desk, staring down at his wallet lying there, thinking on what the hostess had told him, and it all felt wrong.

About half an hour later his phone rang, his private line.

"Mr. Malone?"

It was a woman's voice.

"Who's calling, please?" said Malone.

"I see you got your wallet back."

"You're the one."

"I'm the one... so to speak."

"You should have stayed around… or left your information. I would have given you a reward. I'm happy to give you one now. You can come pick it up, if you like. I'll have a messenger deliver it, if you prefer."

"I'm sure," said Costa.

It got quiet. Both were wading through a silence for their own reasons. Then Malone could hear a garbage truck coming up the street. He could hear it through his apartment windows, and he could hear it in the phone. The call was coming from close by. Very close by.

He grabbed a pair of binoculars from the desk drawer. He went to the window that fronted the street and began a scan. Still neither spoke.

"But that's not what you're after… is it?"

"No," she said. "It isn't."

"You lifted the wallet right when I was at the door having to wait for that skank and her stroller to get past."

She did not answer.

There was a phone booth in front of the bakery. Another down by the corner. Both were empty. Then there was one he could just barely make out on Commerce.

Someone was on the phone. Too many shadows for details, the branches of a tree, broken streams of sunlight.

"Well," he said. "Silence may be golden, but you can't make a goddamn life out of it."

She finally answered. "Lake fuckin' George," she said.

She said it like it was a cool death blow. At least that's how he heard it.

What she heard at that moment was the garbage truck. She heard it loud and clear and close enough to see.

And then she realized—

CHAPTER 166

She was out of the booth and starting down the street, not running, mind you, not doing anything to attract attention, to signal alarm or look suspicious. Just keep an innocent pace and your fingers crossed.

She passed a couple intently into themselves that might give her momentary cover to turn around and she glanced over her shoulder.

She saw he was already out of the building, crossing the street in a sprint to outrun an oncoming cab and its bullying horn. He was the shadow of a man there in the daylight in his charcoal black suit. His head sharply angling left and then right as if on a swivel and there was no doubt he was heading toward the phone booth.

She hadn't even hung up the receiver, she had just dropped it and took off and he saw the receiver was still hanging from its cable and swinging ever so slightly, left and right.

She could not be that far ahead.

At a run he started down Commerce, which was a short, little trafficked street of row apartments, and where Commerce made a sharp curve, there was a theatre, the Cherry Lane Theatre.

Well, there was a crowd by the theatre entrance, and others sitting on stoops or on the curb, pacing the sidewalk, smoking cigarettes and drinking coffee, reading or rehearsing scenes from sheets they carried, pages of scenes they carried, or nervously doing exercises to work off that crazy actor's anxiety.

Malone had been in the neighborhood long enough to know this was an audition in the works. He quit running. The woman who'd called was well around the corner by now and gone, or maybe she was one of the women there. And there must have been about fifty, generally young.

He hadn't seen her well enough through the tree branches and sunlight off the phone booth glass he could even tell you the color of her pants, or were they jeans? And her blouse, it was light, maybe white, or cream, or some putrid shade of yellow.

"You were smart," a voice said.

He turned. It was a youngish woman like most of the others there. She was holding a few pages of script for her audition.

"What?" said Malone.

"You were smart," she repeated. "You come to the audition in that cool looking suit. You'll make a great visual impression."

"Go fuck yourself," he said.

CHAPTER 167

Malone walked back to the apartment building with his hands slumped down in his pants pockets. You'd have thought he was done, he looked done. But he wasn't. He harbored his rage like any good corporate executive should. He'd fucked up getting pickpocketed in a wop bakery, but keep going fella, have lunch, plot the takedown.

He stopped at the phone booth, looked it over, worked it with his thoughts. Then he stared down toward the theatre.

She could have been right there among all those nutcase actors, right there now, not likely, but maybe sitting on the curb, working a smoke, just another bland looking malcontent. But being hooked into either Art Baum or Nat Blue meant she had blood under her fingernails. So… she'd be back.

He searched for a scrap of paper in his coat pockets. Came up with the receipt from that fucking bakery. Wrote on the back:

Phone out of order.
Save your fucking money.

Then he wedged the receipt into the dial for anyone to see.

CHAPTER 168

He made a call from his office and then went back downstairs to the phone booth and waited. Every time he looked at that bakery he cursed under his breath.

A couple of the actors from the audition came cruising up the street, walking past Malone, with those typed up scenes, talking away, all of them just dripping with social relevance and progressive ideology about the Civil Rights movement and voting rights and how plays and music were going to put a righteous end to a generation of racist white men and how the expanding Vietnam War was next on their doom list.

Malone watched them silently as they pontificated with puffed out chests how the system was not going to kidnap their souls or extinguish their dreams.

Then what happened—one of them went into the phone booth and checked the coin return.

About twenty minutes later a nondescript utility truck pulled up and a man with phone repair gear got out.

Malone flashed him an ID.

"Cut the receiver loose at the cable," Malone said. "Get all the fingerprints you can off it. I'm trying to track the last caller."

"You realize it's pretty much a useless task."

Pretty much still leaves a little betting room.

CHAPTER 169

Warsh felt that the demise of the priest might well predict his own future.

"You've been awfully quiet," said Charlie.

"I got the parental blues," said Warsh.

"Yeah… I dig it."

Warsh wondered why they needed three men for this one simply ugly task. But he kept that to himself.

The priest and Avalon were rapping away in French, stumbling over each other's sentences.

"What are you talking about back there?" said Charlie.

"The state of the world. How communists are trying to take over everything. Especially right here in the States. With all these new social progressive ideas that are being pushed. And we got to finance equality. This priest is working it."

Charlie looked into the rearview mirror. Saw Avalon staring back at him.

"He could be one of us," said Avalon.

"But he's not," said Charlie.

CHAPTER 170

They stopped at a Howard Johnson's in Tarrytown. Avalon went in and ordered food to go. The other three waited by the car having a smoke. Avalon made a pit stop in the bathroom on the way out.

While the men ate by the car Avalon got a 16mm Bolex out of the trunk and started filming the scene.

"What's with the film?" said Warsh.

"The priest doesn't get it," said Charlie. "This film will be used to warn his communist friends what happens to those who want to overthrow America."

"What are you talking?" said Warsh. "Malone pentothaled this guy... how many times? He said he was straight up."

"But the pentothal didn't work on him so good," said Charlie. "Some of the information he gave us was good. The rest Malone compared with reports from Laos. This guy is a VC soldier. The real thing. And that's not a good thing. Them being willing to come here and die for the cause like this. They got to be killed and killed soon before they breed."

"We have to get out of here," said Avalon. "I laced his drink with a blowout dose of Lucy and he should start hallucinating pretty soon."

Warsh had no idea. He'd been told nothing of any of this. He was up front now, with Charlie at the wheel staring at him. Warsh kept cool. Waited to see how it would all shake out. After all, Avalon could have dosed him just as easy.

Warsh saw the priest was getting a little squirrelly. His eyes were flashing open and closed, like he was trying to clear his vision. He'd opened the rear window like he needed air. He was holding his chest. His heartbeat must be blasting off from the panic. Who knew what was flashing across his brainwaves?

He leaned forward and shook Avalon's shoulder. "I think I'm unwell," he said in French.

"What is it?" said Avalon.

The priest tried hard to explain what for him would be unexplainable.

CHAPTER 171

They saw the priest was unraveling. It was a horrifying and tragic meltdown. He was trying to scream away the monster confusion in his head, the hallucinations a doorway to madness.

They were along the Hudson River, not far from Lyndhurst mansion, which you could see on a hill in the moonlight.

Charlie pulled up an untended driveway to the abandoned remains of a house and carriage shed.

The car pulled into the shed and the headlights went out. They dragged the priest from the car. Avalon tried to console him. But it was a fraud, of course. They had him on the ground. Charlie tossed a pair of ankle cuffs to Warsh. He began to fight, but Warsh got the priest's spindly legs braced.

He was a sight now. As he began to cry, Charlie cuffed the priest's wrists.

Avalon retrieved the camera and a workman's flashlight from the car. He tossed the light to Warsh.

"Get in close," said Avalon. "Keep the light on his face and chest."

Warsh did as ordered.

With the light on him the priest froze up. He did not understand what was happening but then there was this sudden dire recognition of something. It was as if he understood the nightmare he was living. His screaming became unbearable. It was full out rage.

"What the fuck is he saying?" said Charlie.

"He knows we got him," said Avalon. "For what he is, and he's cursing out the white man."

Avalon filmed him until he was almost all out of negative. He stopped, then to Warsh, he said, "Slit that VC's throat."

PALISADES AMUSEMENT PARK

CHAPTER 172

Bill was in the kitchen eating a very, very old slice of heated up pizza when there was a hard knock at the front door and a voice shouted, "Police… open up… now."

Bill dropped the pizza back onto the plate. Could not figure out what the fuck—

Another hard knock as he made for the front door. More aggressive. And that voice again.

He got a full rush of sunlight and there on the porch was Viola. She was all dished up. Looking mighty good.

"It's five o'clock," she said. "Get yourself together. You're coming with me."

"Where we going?"

"None of your business. Get a move on."

While he went to the bedroom to change she checked out the kitchen. Saw the beer, saw that sorry looking slice of pizza. She picked it up. Thought to take a bite. Smelled it first. Forget it.

When he returned she was at the kitchen table, sitting back and sipping his beer. Her legs up on the table, her silky skirt barely covering those smooth thighs. Very nice, he thought.

Viola looked him over. He was wearing a black T-shirt and black jeans and black boots.

"You're looking like a real hood," she said. "Full of no good and bad boy thoughts."

"I do my best."

"That's how you were dressed the first day we met up at the gas station."

He took the beer from her.

"You actually remember crap like that?"

"It's part of the female gene pool. We remember everything."

"Sounds great," he said, deadpan, then he sipped the beer.

"It has its upsides," she said. "We get to rerun all the wrongs you guys dish out over the years and somewhere down the road we take our revenge."

"That's something to look forward to."

"I think so."

He reached for the pizza. Thought to get in one good bite at least, before they left for wherever they were going.

She slipped it out of his hand.

"What the fuck was that about?" he said.

"Forget that slice of rat bait."

"Why?"

"It smells like old socks… You want to contract ptomaine?"

CHAPTER 173

Viola drove. It was a New York state of mind kind of night. Perfect for windows open wide and radio turned way, way up. The skyline of the city sweeping across the hood of her car. She put a hand out the window.

"It's like feeling the whole universe," she said.

She made like she was catching something that flew past. She then offered Bill that closed fist. When she opened her hand there was a beautifully rolled joint just waiting to be smoked.

"Let's get properly stoned. Not too much—"

"Not too little," he answered.

He lit up. They swapped tokes. Then she said, "Lick my neck, boy."

He licked her neck, like any self respecting outlaw would.

They were kicking it down the Henry Hudson, then onto Riverside Drive and then there it was, the George Washington Bridge looming up out of the night.

"We're going to Jersey," he said.

"How'd you figure that?"

"The George Washington Bridge was a subtle giveaway."

They were properly stoned and sang along with Sam the Sham and the Pharaohs doing Wooly Bully.

There was one downside to all this—Viola destroyed the art of singing.

Palisades Amusement Park sat atop the cliffs on the Jersey side of the Hudson River and faced that eternal New York City skyline.

Cousin Brucie of WABC was one of the most preeminent disc jockeys on AM radio, and he would sponsor hit parade nights at the park, where a host of rock and rollers would perform.

That night playing their hits it was Lou Christie, the Sapphires, the Rip Chords, Barbara Lewis, Dee Dee Sharp, Randy and the Rainbows, Rosie and the Originals—

"I had a reason for bringing you here tonight," said Viola. "It wasn't just on a whim."

CHAPTER 174

They stood at the entrance of the parking lot, beneath a giant neon sign that listed the entertainers that night in the blazing neon.

"See if you can guess why," she said.

She stood there with that stoned smile and slinky skirt watching his eyes fumble around as the crowd flowed by, looking, thinking, lost. This went on long enough for him to smoke a cigarette down to nothing.

"I'm nowhere man," he said.

"I think you're pretty close," she said back.

He didn't know what that meant, but assumed it meant something.

He looked all around him again. He dropped the cigarette butt, killed it with the heel of his boot. And then he got it, or hoped he got it.

There on the black asphalt were the reflected names of the entertainers imprinted in burning neon.

He pointed to one of the names.

"Barbara Lewis," he said.

She had brought him right to it. She had a passionate victory smile.

"That first night," he said.

"After we left the White Horse…"

"Cruising up through the Village…"

"Just us and the world."

"Was the world there… I hadn't noticed," he said.

"Baby, I'm yours…"

"Until…." He put a hand to his ear for her to finish.

"I won't sing it. I don't want to ruin the moment."

"It was something about the end of time," he said.

"Forever, I think," she said. "I think even longer."

He took her by the hand. She slipped an arm under his. She whispered, "I relive that night."

They had danced to that song and like endless generations of first dates, first moments, first memories, born out of a song, it will be with them forever. The forever of love and beauty, and the forever of tragedy and loss.

CHAPTER 175

Malone had gotten word from Avalon by phone. It was an agreed to simple one line to let Malone know about the priest, that all had gone well.

"He boarded the ship," said Avalon.

One job goes down successfully, one is lurking in the darkness. Isn't that always the way of it.

It was a four cocktail night at Chumley's Pub. A sit back in a very dark bar, at a very quiet table, alone. Malone was grabbing for answers. Obsessed by evil thoughts of being on the outside, at being threatened even for a minute.

He had two more drinks at home. He lay in bed in the dark. A man with an ugly tension.

When the phone rang it was like the bell in between rounds in a prizefight.

"Yeah," he said.

It was three in the morning, it was her.

"I have a financial offer for you," she said.

He snaked his way up out of the sheets. He reached for a cigarette on the table beside the bed.

"Tempt me," he said.

"First," she said, "a story."

Oh, when he hears this. Another orphan scam. Maybe it's got teeth, maybe not.

"Back in 1957… You had people… one step removed from the Army… releasing aerosols of drugs in the subways. You used the Bronx lines at one point… The drugs were experimental and illegal… Drugs like Lucy… They also proved to be dangerous, flawed… There were fatal reactions. One of those people was the victim of someone on those drugs… A woman murdered on the Pelham Parkway line."

He slipped his legs off the bed. He stood up.

"I know the man who committed the murder," she said.

He knew she wouldn't be at that same phone, but he went to the window anyway. Looked from the phone she'd called from to the next, and the next.

"Eight years is a long time to carry around such a tale like that… and not profit," said Malone. "Right?"

"Time and circumstances."

"How much do you think time and circumstances are worth?"

"One hundred thousand dollars."

"Reasonably priced," he said. "For about twenty years from now."

"Chumley's is quite the nice bar," she said. "Isn't it?"

This fucking dragon, he thought. *This sleazy, ambitious—*

"You had four drinks there. You looked very pensive. A man with a cross on his back… Or a bull's-eye."

"That's me," he said. "Pensive but very thorough. Torturously so."

"I appreciate men that are thorough."

"I'll bet you do."

"Pensive I can take or leave," she said.

"I can guess why. Those types have you looking over your shoulder. Sweating... The Forever Sweat, I call it."

"By the way, I walked right past you. Right past your table to test your attention. You didn't even look up."

"You should have stopped and said hello."

With that the phone went dead.

CHAPTER 176

Did you ever have sex on the Henry Hudson Parkway? I mean when traffic is flying along after you've passed the GW Bridge?

And just like that, without a word, without a hint, Viola was peeling off her shoes and slipping off that sheer sexy skirt she was inhabiting. From behind the wheel Bill watched her with bad intentions. She'd have stripped off her panties and bra, but she wasn't wearing either.

Bill didn't need to have what was happening explained to him. He'd gotten high marks when it came to Wild and Reckless 101.

She put her foot on the gas pedal and worked the steering wheel while he yanked off his boots, then used an arm to shim out of his jeans. Then he managed his underwear and when he got that done he tossed his Fruit of the Loom out the window in Oscar worthy disregard.

This was the poetry of youth in action. Wild and flamboyant and well beyond good manners. Before they got to it they were laughing over Cousin Brucie who had appeared on stage to emcee the concert wearing a leopard skin tuxedo. I mean from head to foot leopard skin, pants included, shoes included.

This was their foreplay chatter as she climbed onto his lap, the car doing a rumbly sixty up the Henry Hudson. A ride that would keep sex full of surprises, because the Henry Hudson was famous for its potholes.

CHAPTER 177

They lay in bed in his house in the dark, with only a little firefly of burning ash from the tip of a cigarette that passed between them.

"Time for the question," he said out of nowhere.

She eased around a bit. It was not a sleepily asked question.

"What question is that?" she said.

"Tonight," he said.

"Tonight?" she answered.

"Give me the reality."

"It sounds like you're ordering something off a menu."

"I am… The truth over easy, please. Hold the bullshit."

She lifted slightly to rest on one arm. "I feel a terrible shadow coming over the moment."

"Tonight was all about getting me ready."

"For what?" she said.

"You have something on your mind. You had something on your mind. That was what tonight was all about, that something was on your mind. Is still on your mind."

She sat now, the sheet fell away from her naked body.

"My heart was in the right place," she said.

She got up and walked to the bedroom window.

"My body, on the other hand," she said, "was another story altogether."

"The whole night was about getting me out of the city. Blowing this place off."

She leaned against the wall beside the window. Looked out into the empty lot beside the house that flanked the hill up to the Esplanade tracks.

"Warsh isn't back, right?"

"No."

"Neither is my father."

"Not surprising."

"You believe the story Papi told you?"

"No," said Bill.

"I don't believe my father either. I'm getting to know the look when he's lying or brushing me off. You think Papi is a threat?"

"Yeah... I don't want to think so... But I do. What about your father?"

"I think he's at the dark end of The American Street. A street I'm learning about firsthand. Am getting too familiar with. Do you consider Warsh the enemy?"

"I'm afraid it's leaning that way. I don't like it. What about you and your old man?"

"I'm already tipping over. You gonna tell Warsh about the personal ad? Where we're at?"

"Not a chance. You gonna tell your father?"

"He'd put it down. He'd put me down. And somewhere in all that he'd flip out. I'd have turned into the bad seed. No... I'm already the bad seed."

"What about your internship with what's his name?"

"Malone. No way. But who knows where that will go now?"

"I was right," said Bill. "Tonight was all about you smoothing the runway to get me out of this city."

"Yeah… I was gonna hit you with… We could change the world from another zip code. We could make a life somewhere else. My mother left me a trust. You notice I use the word 'we'… We don't have to make the fight from here."

He was across the room and when he spoke, he spoke very quietly but there was resolve in his voice. "I'm not so sure about that."

"That's what I was afraid of."

She ran her fingers across the glass where the rain teared down the window. There was something, a lurking figure anyway, in the deep recess of the darkness at the rear end of the empty lot where the hill went up to the tracks.

"It's not going to get violent," she said.

"Maybe not," said Bill.

She leaned back.

"Tell that to whoever is watching the house."

CHAPTER 178

He pressed against the bedroom wall and looked out to where she pointed.

He saw nothing.

But standing there, time was wasting.

He rushed from the bedroom and down the hall to the closet.

She was right behind him as he put on a slicker. He scrambled to get his boots on after that. He cut some damn figure at the breakfront.

"What are you going to do?" she said.

He removed a handgun from the breakfront top drawer. He made sure the weapon was loaded.

She tried to stop him.

It was useless and foolish.

"This is exactly what I didn't want," she said.

"Then you should have said nothing."

He was hustling back up the hall to the kitchen and then to the laundry room where the back door was.

Viola tried to stop him again before he slipped out into the night.

She was cursing herself.

"Maybe it was nothing," she said.

"And maybe it wasn't," he said.

And then he was gone.

He moved along the backyard fence, vines and undergrowth had grown up through the chain links.

He could see pretty far into the empty lot. There were dopers back there sometimes, drunks, kids hanging out, hiding out, plotting their crazy scenarios, but tonight there was nothing... so far.

There was an old gate and it made that rusty sound old gates do when he opened it.

He stared out into the empty lot. He hadn't even closed his slicker and it flapped open as he moved and did he cut a figure.

Bronx resident naked in the rain gets arrested... almost naked anyway.

He heard something behind him. He turned to find it was Viola barefoot and wrapped in a sheet.

"Maybe I was wrong," she said.

She looked at the gun at his side, she looked at the determination in his expression.

"You're not afraid, are you?"

"Why should I… I've been killed once already."

It was a dark and ugly statement of fact that had led to other dark and ugly statements of fact that ultimately led to this moment, with two outliers in the world standing in a soon to be swampy trash laden lot with the subway passing in a flash of lights and windows.

"Let's go inside," said Viola, "before you have to use that."

"You wanted me to be out here, otherwise you would never have said anything at all. You wanted to know."

"Maybe," she said. "I don't know. I can be foolish. Maybe there's nothing out here and we should just go."

"Maybe it's your father out there," said Bill.

"If that doesn't send a chill up my back… nothing ever will."

The lights along the rainy tracks were an unwelcome scene of gloom.

"What if it was Warsh?" said Viola.

"I actually thought it might be him. Putting the fear of God into us."

Bill then shouted, "I'll hunt you out. Be warned!"

CHAPTER 179

The day started out bad for Malone and proceeded to get worse. The privately sourced agent handling the fingerprints on the pay phone receiver had come up empty.

Malone was detailing everything about the conversation he'd had with this unsourced, unnamed woman when an aide appeared in the doorway of Malone's office.

"Yes," said Malone.

The aide was holding an envelope.

"This is for you, sir."

"Bring it here."

He did. Malone looked the envelope over. He saw his name was written in script. There was no address, no return address, and no stamp.

"Where did you get this?"

"It was left under the door, sir."

"What door?"

"The outer office door upstairs."

"When?"

"It had been slipped under the door by the time I arrived."

Malone got straight up and started for the window to see outside, then he thought—the hell with that.

He excused the aide and opened the envelope. And what does he find—a personal ad cut from a Bronx newspaper soliciting information about an unsolved murder on the Pelham Parkway line back in June of 1957. The name of the victim—Warsh.

FIFTH AVENUE

CHAPTER 180

In the envelope had also been a copy of the original newspaper article detailing the murder. The article, in the *Bronx Press*, also included an artist's rendering of the murder, as put together by a half dozen witnesses.

Malone laid all this out on his desk including his notes on the phone call with this unknown and unsourced woman.

He left everything as it was until Avalon arrived. The first words out of Malone were "We have a disaster on our hands."

Avalon pulled a chair up to the desk and sat. He scanned everything that Malone had laid out.

"What I am about to tell you," said Malone, "goes nowhere beyond you. Especially Charlie Dash and Warsh. Put a red flag over both their names… Both of them are on the outside of this. Also… I have someone looking into Warsh and his nephew."

Avalon studied everything while Malone gave him a play by play of what he knew, what he surmised, what had been laid on him, what plagued hum, concerned him, what could bring down this whole operation.

Was the woman at Lake George with Art Baum or Nat Blue. Avalon was sure it was Art Baum.

The original artist's sketch of the murderer only marginally looked like Baum. And now that he was dead, there was little to nothing they could legally lay blame at the Malone operational doorstep. But as for the woman—

What plagued Malone the worst—the unanswered question—who was behind the ad. Was it the unnamed and unsourced woman, or someone else. Maybe Warsh, maybe his nephew. And if it was them—

There was a phone number attached to the ad.

He was thinking—how best to shrink this secret down to size.

CHAPTER 181

Rick entered Malone's apartment. He could see into Malone's private office that he was busy. Malone saw Rick and waved the youth in. He introduced Rick.

"My young radical friend here and I," said Malone, "need a few private minutes."

Avalon left glancing at that host of information on the desk as he went. He quietly shut the door behind him.

"How's surveillance going?" said Malone.

"The Dash girl and Warsh's nephew are tight. I don't see father and daughter on the same wavelength. Very iffy. Especially when it comes to the younger Warsh. He's hardcore. I see trouble. And she looks like she can dish it out as well as take it. I've seen Viola and Warsh more than once at an attorney's office over on Bronxwood and Mace."

"A private home?"

"Yeah."

"By Saint Lucy's Grotto?"

"Yeah."

"Well dressed guy… Handsome."

"And queer."

"Gardner Flynn… Don't fuck with him."

"No?"

"He's got contacts in government a mile high. Every closet case, every Mafia closet case, goes to him."

CHAPTER 182

The first wave of protestors was collecting at Mount Morris Park along Fifth Avenue, right there at the border of Harlem. Flags had been set up atop the old stone watchtower, built during the Revolutionary War as an outpost for patriots. There were United States flags and flags with peace symbols and others that said Voting Rights Now.

There were about a hundred ralliers, a lot of them carrying placards and squares of white sheet that spoke to the cause. The march was to take Fifth Avenue straight down, past Central Park and the Boathouse and onto Grand Central Station… If they made it that far.

It was not a march to tempt lawlessness. But they knew that the lawless would come their way. Word had leaked out. Not everyone was committed to Voting Rights. Not equality either, and certainly not equity. It was a racial thing and not a racial thing at the same time. It was just as much about class. About who you put in public office, about who gets to set the rules of the road. And that road always comes with violence. Dallas and the Texas Book Depository taught everyone that much. The Audubon Ballroom was another such chapter. Then there was Ford's Theatre. Even when things go right, they're dragging what's wrong along with them.

Word came down and they started hitting the street. Right then a hand came to rest on Viola's shoulder.

It was Rick.

"I need to steal a minute of your time," he said.

He sounded serious, and she mentioned that.

He nodded he was. He took her aside. They were rushing past her, the protestors, and starting down Fifth Avenue.

"I have something you need to know," he said, "and what I'm going to tell you cannot be spoken of. This conversation cannot have happened."

"Hey, man," she said. "Where are you going?"

"You're under surveillance… You're being watched."

"Me…?"

"Yeah. You."

"By who?"

"By Malone."

She stopped right there, arched her back.

"Me… why?"

"I can't for sure answer that."

"Can't… or won't."

"Can't."

"How do you know then?"

"I'm the one he ordered to watch you."

"You have to be shitting me."

He was being shouted to from across the street. His crew was waiting on him.

"Later," he said, as he sprinted across Fifth.

She was shouting after him, "You can't just leave me like this."

"But I am," he said.

CHAPTER 183

She was being swept up into America at every turn. An America she could not now completely fathom or fully understand. The pawn with the heart of gold had little on her.

God only knows. She was being played, she knew that much.

This was a time of duplicity and doubt, and the trappings of goodness and justice hadn't yet come to the rescue. Conflict was year round, it wasn't like the holidays, here for a few hungry weeks then packed away till next year.

She and one group of protestors were headed down the west side of Fifth Avenue and another group with Rick as one of its leaders walked the other.

They were carrying placards and posters and they handed out fliers to whomever that passed. At every stoplight they swarmed into the streets offering cabbies and truckers and delivery men, businessmen and people of every stripe and circumstance, handbills for upcoming rallies and fundraisers for voting rights.

They were reaching out to that silent majority asking them to honk their horns if they were into the cause.

They forged up with another group that was passing out fliers on the sidewalk by the reservoir and putting flags up on the Boathouse roof. There were dozens more who were rallying in front of the Museum of Modern Art that joined them. At the corner the protestors on the other side of Fifth that Rick was part of crossed over. They were one massive army of marchers, bucking traffic, working the lights, heading down Fifth, leaving a trail of horns honking behind them.

Of course, this was the real world, so it wasn't all a Ringling Brothers bromide of love and social progress. There were plenty of the old tropes being spewed out at the marchers. A lot of it was the work of the time worn "fuck you" crowd… the "Go back to Puerto Rico, spic" crowd… the "sambo hater" crowd that promised marchers they'd never get the vote….

Then of all things, at the corner by the museum, a marcher, an older woman, a real teacher, got hit in the back of the neck with a shoe. From out of nowhere a discount Florsheim bounced off the crest of her spine.

A couple of kids up the sidewalk broke out laughing and took off. And there was this one time public servant who was holding a shined shoe, and telling anyone who passed, "Someone threw a shoe at me... a good shoe... one shoe... what's the point of throwing one shoe."

Viola was doing double duty passing out fliers and taking snapshots. She got one of a cabbie who just as the light changed opened his driver's door and sped off through the intersection and tagged a protestor with the door and sent him down the pavement like he was a pool ball.

CHAPTER 184

The march never got to 42nd Street, it never got to Grand Central Station. It got no further than that street corner, no further than that cab.

The cab got hung up in a traffic jam at the intersection. A couple of protestors had already laid chase after it. The kid who got bowled was up now, alive and alert and ready to kick ass. He charged the cab, other marchers were already banging on the hood and windows and trying to get the doors open.

The cabbie was ready to party and came out of the vehicle wielding a tire jack, shouting he wasn't about to take crap from a bunch of fag liberals.

The march had quickly dissolved into an assault of condemnation and insults, filthy language and fists, violence and more violence. A couple of lean brawlers who carried knives and razors, real street crap, charged the crowd, and there was a police siren in the distance.

Protestors were scattering, passersby doing the same, car horns demanding an escape lane, a protest flag lying in the street. But the fighting was gathering impact anyway, impact and import. And not just for flat out human violence, but for the unchecked grievances from all social and political quarters, from all possible states of mind and points of view. This mob of sudden violence was becoming a stand in for the larger context it existed in. She was watching America kill itself on the road to recovery. It came to her just like that.

CHAPTER 185

She watched the depredations of a culture that would be detailed and telecast by the likes of Walter Cronkite and Huntley and Brinkley in gritty television black and white. There would be footage of people bleeding, of marchers being beaten with a trash can, a youth would be on the ground being stomped, being clubbed with a placard, a bloody flag would be caught in a gutter updraft. God Bless America… You hope.

She could imagine the footage of this for years and years. It would become a grim reminder when seen from the ramparts of time. A horror show revived, reconstructed in books and films, and God only knows where and whatever else depending on the outcome of our vested hatreds.

Is there room for decency on the open market of the law?

There was much that was painful pouring out of her. She had become one of them all before she even realized it. Before she pressed her way into the mob around the cab trying to separate combatants, as enraged as she was at being demeaned, being insulted, threatened, at being spit on. Fuckin' spit on.

They may be old tropes, but they still work, they still cut deep, they still hit that human mark and bring grievances to the surface ready for confrontation.

She was pulling at people's arms, at their shirts, getting between one then another, trying to overcome the chaos, trying to make a case, trying to fight back, when something hit the side of her head and there was a flash of light about the size of a garbage can lid.

Moments later she and the asphalt were face to face. Her nose was oozing blood. For how long she lay there she had no idea. Somewhere a police car siren was closing in. People scattered, jumping over the wounded, around the dazed. She saw it all in swimmy burning daylight. Then she was being lifted up.

She thought it was probably one of the marchers until handcuffs were slapped on her.

CHAPTER 186

Gardner's assistant entered his office.

"There's a woman on your private line," she said.

He had a pretty fair idea who it was.

"I'll take it," he said.

It was the Costa woman.

"Can I steal five minutes of your time?" she said.

He checked his watch. "Now?"

"Now."

"Speak away."

"I'll be in the catacombs across the street."

She hung up. She had no intention of this being a discussion.

The catacombs were on the grounds of Lourdes of America. They were a replica of the tombs in ancient Rome. There were scenes created in those tombs. Life size replicas from the life of Christ, the life of saints. There were racks upon racks of candle holders with slots for a bit of change from the faithful.

He walked the catacombs but she was nowhere to be found. He started back up the meandering passage, confused, then there she was in a quiet corner where the shadows were deepest and she could see him before being seen.

She was smoking a cigarette and flicking away its ash and brother did she seem out of place there.

"I didn't live far from here when I was growing up," she said. "And when my mother decided I deserved a beating I'd haul it the hell down here. My mother feared this place. Creeped her out. Too much of the dead. So… I'd have a couple of cigs and wait her out. Oh, I'd still get a beating, bless her bitch of a soul, but it was never quite as bad. I wasn't at one with God and the holy saints… bottom line."

"I don't have time to listen to you reminisce about your life," said Gardner.

"I threatened Mr. Malone," she said.

"You didn't."

"He knows who I am now. And what I'm about. I asked him for one hundred thousand dollars… demanded it, really."

"He'll never pay it."

"Then he'll die with his pride intact."

"He can't pay you and survive."

"I need your help in that regard, as the go between"

"He will kill you. He will have people hunting you already."

"I wasn't going to come to you with this. Because I know there are conflicts and dangers and then something went down today that I believe will force you to help me."

CHAPTER 187

She had a story to tell. A story to exploit Gardner further with.

She dropped her cigarette on the catacomb floor and ground it out with the stub of her heel. Then Costa quieted down as a woman and her two small children walked past, blessing themselves as they came upon a diorama of the centurions walking a bloodied and cross carrying Christ on his trial to Calvary.

Once they were again alone Gardner said, "Get on with it."

And that she did.

Beonca Costa had gone to the gas station on Pelham Parkway to have a clandestine talk with the kid. She intended to tell him about her demand from Malone for the money, and could the kid help her take Malone down, knowing this would have to be done eventually, if the kid expected to ever live a long and safe life. And the girl too… her fate was in the boy's hands. And Costa was willing to give up a nice piece of change from the one hundred thousand dollars for a little blood being shed.

She was watching the kid from the sidewalk just up the street waiting for the right moment… Well…. It came. But totally unexpected. It was as if God had looked down on her and dropped a favor in her mercenary lap.

Because a car pulled into the station and parked by the office and a man got out. And who should that man be?

Costa had no idea who he was by name… But she recognized him. He was the man who had done a walk through of the bus station in Lake George after the killings. He was one of the men she had seen in front of the cabin doing the killing. He was the one who had charged after her when the killing was done. He was the one by the boat in those chukka boots.

Warsh and the kid talked a while, then Warsh got back into his car and pulled out of the station. Beonca Costa took a chance and walked down the sidewalk and right past him, close enough to be seen, to see that Warsh needed a shave and was smoking a nonfilter cigarette.

He looked past her. If he saw her, he sure did not have any idea of her.

CHAPTER 188

They walked the catacombs side by side.

"The boy doesn't know, does he?"

Gardner did not answer that. But his non answer was answer enough.

"Warsh is a murderer," said Costa. "He is one of Malone's people. People who work for a dangerous arm of the Army. The denizens of dirty tricks, dirty acts, illegal acts, all in the service of God and country. He is a Handyman… that's what Art used to call them, including himself… the Handymen. And it was only a compliment if you saw it from their track record of efficiency.

She took a step closer, literally invading Gardner's personal space.

"They were spraying aerosols of Lucy in the subways," she said. "Or feeding it to suckers. Maybe like Art Baum. He might have been dosed the same day. And who was working that program… Warsh. His actions could have directly, or indirectly, led to his sister's murder. How's that for a tale to tell Billy the kid?"

They were standing in the grotto, surrounded by statues of the saints and the angels and holy moments of faith. Gardner lit a cigarette. He did not offer the woman one. So she asked. He did so with cool dispatch.

"It would be a bitch," she said, "to have your pocket picked. I want you to just help me safely make the trade for the money. We tell the kid nothing. I tell the kid nothing. I pass over half the money to him and the girl. I'm gonna kill Malone anyway... in my own fashion."

He stared at her, he smoked, then he went and sat on a grotto bench. He watched people come and go to the shrine of Lourdes with bottles and jugs to collect holy water.

Costa came and sat near him on the bench.

Gardner pointed his cigarette toward the shrine, where water poured forth from a mechanical spring just below the feet of the holy lady.

"It's not actually holy water from Lourdes," he said. "It comes from a city tap. People know that. But it gives people hope, gives them faith, a reason to be, that God may hear them and come to their aid."

He pointed his cigarette now where crutches and wheelchairs were left as a sign of people who had been healed. And where pictures had been left by souls who had been to this place and found some degree of peace, if not peace itself.

"Does all this mean you're going to help me?" said Beonca. "Or do I go and tell the kid what I know?"

"I have an alternative version of how this story plays out," said Gardner. "Maybe you'd like to hear it?"

SERIOUS LAND

CHAPTER 189

She was dragging when she got back home, and the side of her head hurt pretty much. She'd returned to gather up a back seat worth of clean clothes and bring them over to Bill's place.

The house was completely dark, her father's car partly up on the grass, which meant he was loaded up.

She didn't want to wake him so she entered through the patio and went right to the kitchen. She made herself a sandwich out of leftovers and snagged a beer and sat in the darkness and ate.

She replayed the events of the day and considered the state of her life. In the short time since she had returned, the world she knew, or thought she knew, and the world she anticipated were gone for good. Like that science fiction book she was the *Stranger in a Strange Land*… And maybe… just maybe… she had knowingly come to the truth of this land.

She had passed through some kind of American façade where all the rules and their bylaws were in play, to get her first full taste of demons in suits, with their hard working compatriots.

With an angry spirit Viola wondered not where do you go from here, but how do you get to where you mean to go from here.

And it's not those blurred shadows that are the most sinister and treacherous, but the clear sharp lines that mean to divide and conquer the world we all live in.

Viola was sitting there, deep in what she called "serious land," sipping on her beer, when she heard this woman's sudden laughter, drunkish almost, coming from somewhere upstairs. A very irksome kind of laugh, closing in on Viola's solitude.

A moment later there was a naked, middle aged woman in the half moonlight of the hallway who came to a dead stop when she spotted a girl in shadow sitting at the kitchen table.

The woman made a funky, embarrassed sound.

"I wonder," said Viola, "which of us is more shocked."

"Who are you?" said the woman.

"Aren't I supposed to ask you that?"

"You're the daughter."

"I'm the incorrigible, yes, and you're naked."

Then to add a little chaser to this cocktail of a moment, a voice out of the hallway said, "Kiki... where are you, girl?"

"Right here," said Kiki. "I'm talking with your—"

Charlie walked right into the scene. Naked as the day he was born. And not a flattering picture either. Viola closed her eyes and her father heard her say, "Oh God... How depressing."

CHAPTER 190

They got the scene straightened up, the woman dressed, Charlie too. And after a few pitiful apologies and some coma inducing chitchat Charlie herded the woman into a cab, prepaid the driver, and good-bye. Kiki went into the sleeping night and her next trick.

Once alone Charlie went over to his daughter who was washing her dish. He took hold of her face to check it out. He had spotted the welty bruise.

"Let's ice that up," he said.

He went to the refrigerator for an ice tray and towel from the drawer to wrap the ice in.

"What happened?" he said. "You mouth off to somebody."

"Something like that."

He wrapped a handful of ice in the towel and set it on the counter by the sink.

"Well," he said. "How did it happen?"

"The rally on Fifth Avenue," she said.

"Rally? You mean riot."

"If you want to call it that… riot," she said.

"Figures," he said. "It's been all over the news."

"I'll have to check it out… see if it made Cronkite."

"Sure… It's just a fuckin' joke. It's all a joke."

She picked up the towel with the ice wrapped in it.

"I got arrested, by the way," she said.

He shook his head.

"Arrested?" he said.

"A couple of undercover characters claimed I started a fight with a cab driver, but—"

"Claim… fight?"

"It was debatable… I was jumped. Got knocked out."

"How did you get bailed out?"

"I was released on my own recognizance… thanks to Gardner."

"Gardner? How did he get involved?"

"How do you think?"

"Surprise me."

"I needed a lawyer."

Charlie was discouraged and mad.

She was going to tell her father not to sweat it, but she knew there was worse to come.

"A source that works your side of the street told me that you and

Warsh were both considered real bad asses… in the trade, so to speak. And that hell was going to rain down on you both… someday."

Charlie Dash looked as if he had been struck a blow dutifully served that one could die from.

"What… the trade? Who the fuck…? What's going on here? You think you're some kind of street angel, is that it…? You're not."

CHAPTER 191

After getting out of jail Viola had not proceeded straight home. Instead, she had driven up to Spanish Harlem. It was not a pretty neighborhood. Lots of poverty there, and no shortage of rage.

As a matter of fact there were generations of poor there, generations of wounded, soul battered people. That was for sure. Many of them had lived down in Lincoln Square until the likes of John D. Rockefeller and Robert Moses politely confiscated the land and ran the people out so they could create the Lincoln Center.

She remembered. Her father had taken her to that neighborhood on the day returning from the Warsh house right after the boy's mother had been murdered. The day she met that boy, Billy Warsh, while sitting in that blue Lincoln.

All those years later and that world and its lies and duplicities were still circling in around her—and them all. The crushing weight of that reality to replay and replay and replay with only different lies and different duplicities to guide them.

Her destination was a second floor walkup just off 110th Street. Kids were playing on the stairs, Spanish kids. She found the apartment and knocked on the scarred up door. There was music coming down from the darkish hallway.

A woman in a nurse's outfit answered. She looked Viola over. Asked her in Spanish what she wanted.

Viola answered back in Spanish. "I'm here to see—"

Rick stepped into view. "What are you doing here?"

"I have questions that need answering."

Rick invited her in. Introduced her to the nurse, who, it turned out, spoke English and was Rick's aunt. There was a second woman in the tiny kitchen, cooking, also an aunt. And a third woman who was bedridden. This was Rick's mother. She waved to Viola weakly.

"MS," whispered Rick.

The aunt in the kitchen who did not speak English well asked Viola if she would like some quesitos and black tea. Viola answered in Spanish she would, very much so.

Viola saw a small quarter of living room had been draped off for a desk and bed. "You all live here?"

"Yeah."

"Three women and one bathroom."

"It's challenging," said Rick.

The aunt in the kitchen had set the table.

"We'll take it up on the roof," said Rick.

CHAPTER 192

They walked to the roof. They sat on the ledge. They drank their tea, and picked at their pastries. From there you could look down into the soul of Manhattan, with all its legacies of unfairness and hatred. They cut quite the contrary image at that moment. On top of that, Rick was uncomfortably quiet, until he said, "You acquitted yourself pretty well today."

"I don't remember," she said.

"You bloodied some guy's mouth."

"I had no idea... I was in a daze... Now... Let's get on with it."

"You want to know why you're being watched," he said.

"That's a fair introduction to a relevant conversation."

"From what I picked up it has something to do with a couple of murders up in Lake George. You know about that?"

"I recall my father talking about it."

"They're after a woman. Who might be involved. I don't know why. But something bad is going to happen."

"How do you know that?"

"They've gone outside the office... Malone, anyway... to recruit someone to take charge and see the search for this woman through."

Viola was going to ask the question—about who the woman was. Then she hesitated. What if this were some kind of ploy, plot, or plan of action that was being exacted against her to get her to open up about Costa, to let them know she knew her.

"I'm warning you to be careful."

"It was you," said Viola.

"Me... what?"

"It was you in the rain the other night. At the Warsh house on Matthews Avenue."

No matter what he said, she saw he was guilty. And at his very worst, half heartedly honest.

"I'm ashamed to admit it. But I was ordered."

"Why did you tell me at all?"

"I think you can guess."

She could. She stood. She took her cup and her plate. This conversation was over.

"I've been here long enough to know one thing with these people," he said.

"And what's that?"

"Our honesty is always in question."

"Not mine," she said.

CHAPTER 193

"I've got something to tell you," said Gardner. "And I'm gonna be blunt and it's gonna be bad."

Gardner had told Bill nothing more. Bill arrived at the house on Bronxwood and Mace in the middle of the night. Gardner had made coffee. The kid wasn't interested. Gardner offered the kid a drink. The kid wasn't interested. All he was, was pissed.

"I thought you were gonna be blunt," said Bill.

"It's a matter of prepping you," said Gardner.

"I'm prepped. I filled my gas tank. I checked the oil. And my tires' air pressure is good. Now… fucking get to it."

Gardner told Bill about the conversation with Costa that he had. It wasn't a conversation really. It was a threat disguised as a conversation. And that threat was a stab to the youth's heart.

Costa, it seems, had been at the Warsh gas station the day before to confront Bill. To lay some bad truth on him that would help her get the money she was after. But when Bill showed with Warsh, that changed everything.

Beonca had recognized Bill's uncle right away. He was one of the two shooters at Lake George. He was the man who had laid chase after her. The one she spotted searching the bus depot not long afterward.

The other shooter with him, she could not identify except to say he was heavyset and middle aged, balding, and sloppy. The kid knew whose description that fit.

Costa meant to have the money she demanded from Malone and she'd sink the ship, and everyone in it, in order to see this through.

CHAPTER 194

Bill paced the dining room. He paced the den that looked out upon the grotto with Gardner waiting in the doorway. Even in that subdued light the kid's expression was a seething life trail. He looked at Gardner, studied him. Gardner slipped his hands into his pockets and just waited.

"I knew we were getting to this as a possible for quite a while now," said Bill. "You don't happen to have a miracle in your pocket, do you?"

"No, son... I don't. But I'm working on it."

"Good... because I know you're just about to lay on me the kill shot."

The way the youth had said it, Gardner knew.

"How do you know that?" said Gardner.

"You have your hands in your pockets. Whenever you change gears from serious to dire, your hands slip into your pockets. Probably to clench your fists."

"Very observant."

"Your uncle and Charlie were, for a time, in operational charge of experimental drugs being aerosoled on the subway against unknowing citizens... Lucy predominantly... or LSD, as the street cool call it. They were in charge of unleashing it on the subway... the Pelham Parkway line... the day your mother was killed, and you, almost so."

"He wasn't on the subway that day. He was at the garage."

"True. But he oversaw Art, as did Charlie... so one could say they were all indirectly responsible."

In that youth's expression Gardner saw something die. And Bill could not lean heavily on willpower to make it disappear, because his past was being dismantled. Being turned from the tragic into something incomprehensibly so.

"Not even a whisper," said Bill. "Not after all these years. Not even when he was drunk, and it might slip out."

"You're questioning Costa's veracity. It's possible."

The youth looked broken hearted.

Bill started to leave.

"Don't go home," said Gardner.

"Got to go sooner or later."

"Later might be better."

"Maybe not."

"You might be less… enraged."

"I want to be enraged."

Gardner waited in the den. At the front door he heard a loud thud. It sounded like something taking its life out on the wall.

CHAPTER 195

Bill drove home in the middle of a hazy Bronx night. A telling Bronx night, on Matthews Avenue, anyway. He had a hard time envisioning it now as home—the truth carried a lot of ugly around with it now.

You cannot make it right, you can only make it different.

He was getting a crash course in the deep dark secrets of the country he lived in. Can you give enough blood to affect the outcome, change the outcome. What if there's not enough blood in the world?

He drove with the radio off. It was only the outside world sneaking in.

He had no idea Viola would be there, at the house, on the porch, in the dark, cigarette in hand, barefooted and nervous, scared really.

Gardner had called her at home. It was not long after she had her conversation with her father. Gardner told her what was going down, that Bill would be at Gardner's home shortly... for the talk. And that she better get to his house to keep Bill from his uncle... If she could.

His headlights flared over her. She was up damn fast as he pulled into the driveway. A screech of brakes and tire rubber announced his return as he pulled into the driveway. Her intention—to deliver him from anything crazy. If she could.

He came storming out of his car like something drawn in broad strokes. He saw her making straight for him down the porch steps.

"Gardner, right... right?"

"He called me... yeah."

Bill wrapped a hand around her jaw. Saw what the wound told him. "This is not your day," he said.

"Don't do anything crazy."

"You mean like everybody else."

"Something you'll regret. I'll regret. Something that will hold you down, hold you back."

She tried to physically stop him from taking the stairs up to Warsh's place.

Bill could not be stopped. He was running on high octane energy and literally lifted her out of his way and plopped her back down.

Bill was carrying one terrible grief in that lean, angry body with enough pain to kill a perfectly reliable heart.

Possessed by a vendetta now he could feel violence pounding away in him and spitting out the words:

There is nothing worse than having your trust destroyed. You are left with nothing more to say.

She was pulling on his shirt up those second floor steps. She was shouting to Warsh to get out. If he was even there. He hadn't answered when she rang the bell earlier.

CHAPTER 196

Warsh had heard her.

Gardner had called. One of those middle of the night never good news phone calls.

"I hope you understand," said Gardner. "I had to do it. He's more important than—"

"I know when a ship is sinking. Almost before it starts to go down," said Warsh. "I've been rehearsing my speech."

After he got off the phone he went to the breakfront in the hallway and opened the top drawer. He set aside some Christmas table napkins. Beneath them is where he kept a gun. He checked to see if it was loaded.

Headlights appeared in the street. A car pulled up front. A door slammed. He slipped back down the hallway. There was a kick at the front door. It was Viola.

"Warsh… I know you're in there, man. I need to talk with you. Before something crazy happens, Warsh."

He said and did nothing and was somewhat ashamed, but thought it wiser. Hoped anyway. He set the gun on the kitchen table.

He went over to the counter and started to pour himself a drink 'cause he knew the kid was coming. He'd be emotionally blasting away. He felt like he'd stumbled into an old western.

He looked at the bottle and suddenly did not like the way the bottled looked. Having a drink right now felt like an act of cowardice. Like he needed the false courage booze gives you. He slid it away just as the front door came wildly swinging open.

WHAT I BELIEVE

CHAPTER 197

Bill called out to Warsh in a blood curdling voice. The kid stalking from one room to the next. Warsh heard him, he heard the torture in that voice once before—the day the kid's mother had been murdered. It was a terrible voice, and an omen if ever there was one, and Warsh felt like he was slipping through a crack in the universe, an unforgiving, unyielding, unending crack in the universe he could never put back together again.

Bill charged from room to room. Living room... family room. Viola kept right behind him. Out of breath, no matter. Tearing at Bill's shirt, no matter. Yelling to an unseen Warsh to get out if he was still in the house, no matter.

Then Bill was in the kitchen doorway.

He stood there stone still staring at his uncle. An out of breath Viola clutched Bill's shoulder.

Bill stared at his uncle, who said nothing. Bill saw the whiskey bottle on the counter. And the gun… saw that too on the kitchen table, next to an ashtray with a burning cigarette.

Viola was pleading not just to Warsh, but to Bill. Begging them not to do anything crazy. She tried to break past Bill and get to the weapon herself.

"If I'm not given that gun," she said, "I'm going to call the police."

She kept on, no matter. Warsh got up and tore the phone from the wall and chucked it across the room. It shattered on the floor. It was now just ruined plastic and fingery wire.

"Fuck the phone," he said.

He then sat back down.

"Well?" said Bill.

"Well what?" said his uncle.

"Are you going to lie to me?" shouted Bill. "If you are… Get it on."

"I'm not going to lie to you."

"Tell me a story then. A trumped up story… Like the ones you've been dicking me with all these years."

"Sorry… no trumped up stories tonight."

CHAPTER 198

Then Warsh got to it.

"I'll say what I always say. What I think. What I believe. We have been and are doing a service for this country. Of course, you don't know it. We like to think of ourselves as the family you never see." He looked to Viola. "And that includes your father too.

"On a clear sunny day," he said, "when truth is in the air… we're the family you'd never have over for dinner. Or for the holidays.

That's because the water we swim in is too damn dark and polluted with communists and socialists and American culture haters... Yeah... People who are Russian... North Vietnamese... North Koreans... Chinese... South America trash and their petty dictatorships. People that need to be rooted out and put down. Pretty ugly, ain't it. No medals, thank you.

"And thank God for people like Charlie and me... on our best days."

He took up his cigarette, smoked, then tossed it into the sink. He noted the shocked and disgusted look both Bill and Viola harbored.

"But there are other days... Where we went over the speed limit, so to speak. Crossed the line. Bit off more than we could chew. Missed the mark. Abused the privilege.

"We live with that and go on until we lapse into obscurity and death... With all our achievements and atrocities intact."

He looked from one to the other. With unrepentant eyes.

"Wel... how's that, kids?"

"Oh, Warsh," said Viola. "That sounds like something my father would say. But not you."

"You want to be part of the country and what it is... you want to better it. It's feast or famine."

CHAPTER 199

"And what about this?" said Bill. "Where does this fall?"

Bill was holding a snapshot taken from the refrigerator door where it had been held there for over a decade by a fading New York Yankees hat magnet.

The image was from the treasure trove of the Warsh past. There was Warsh and Bill's mother at Orchard Beach arm in arm and a six year old Billy peeking out from between them.

The image was not flashy beautiful. As a matter of fact it was not special or interesting in any way. It had spidery cracks in spots and the thin white border on those snapshots was discolored from years of human smudges.

"No answer," said Bill. "Just empty sound."

"I can see the trial now," said Warsh. "I was not on the train, Your Honor. And there is only the word of some pickpocket extortionist to condemn me."

"I don't know you," said a horrified Bill.

"You know me… Oh, yeah… You know me. I come with the furnishings and I'm providing you with a truth… Maybe not the unvarnished all time truth. But truth nonetheless."

Bill took a step toward Warsh holding out the photo. Viola saw the kid's shadow pass over the weapon. Dear God, she thought. She asked Bill to let this go, because she knew—

"Yeah, you know me," said Warsh.

"What do I know?"

"I'll sacrifice my personal life for this country. Even if it means losing my sister… Which I wasn't responsible for… God forgive me."

CHAPTER 200

Before Viola could get a sound out of her mouth Bill had lunged at Warsh. Warsh swiped at the weapon. He could have had it, but he didn't get to it clean. The kid was too fast.

Bill had charged him so hard the table went over, the weapon went with it. It spun across the linoleum floor. And there was an uncle and nephew, surrogate father and son in what was becoming a true beat down.

From the door Viola screamed, pleaded, begged, demanded, threatened they stop this before someone died.

Warsh had been driven back against the stove. But he got the first lick in. You could hear across the room the thud his fist made. Bill had been doubled over, dropped to his knees.

But the youth had rage going for him and came on like a cat. He wrapped his arms around Warsh's legs and he pulled.

Warsh's legs came out from under him. He lost his balance and fell backward. His arms grabbed at the air for something, anything to slow the fall.

Too little, too late. The back of his skull hit the edge of the stove. Hit it so hard the flesh was sheared open. And there was blood. Blood spatter all down the white stove and the collar of Warsh's shirt.

Warsh was dazed. Bill was looking for the gun. It had ended up by the refrigerator. Bill threw the table aside to get at it. Warsh had recovered enough and he bludgeoned the kid with a fist and an arm right between the shoulder blades. It took the air out of him alright.

Viola tried to get to the weapon. She was in Warsh's path. He yelled for her to get aside. He grabbed her by the shirt when she would not and tossed her like nothing toward the doorway.

Warsh saw the kid was reaching for the weapon and Warsh kicked Bill in the ribs. Warsh kicked him once, kicked twice, kicked him again and again when Viola wrapped herself around him. She was crying but enraged.

Bill was flat on the floor now and Warsh, even with the weight of that girl on his back, shouldered down.

The three of them were tight together. Everything happening so fast, so surreally. Warsh could not reach the gun. He couldn't get hold enough of Bill's arm to fight the weapon loose, because Viola had a grip that was steadfast around Warsh's neck.

Warsh was choking. He was cursing Viola out for her to come loose. And for a moment his grip slipped, and he lost any advantage he might have been able to have. But the kid had no such bad luck.

He was moving on sheer adrenaline. No time for decisions. Everything was immediate. His arm snaked up then snaked loose just enough. His arm angled so the weapon eyed right at his uncle's skull. The blood from the wound running down through his hair, his neck, his shirt, his cheek. Life and death became interchanged in an instant.

Bill fired.

CHAPTER 201

Viola screamed out.

There was a dead click as the hammer struck.

The gun had not fired.

Bill was sure he had killed his uncle. He had charged headlong into an act of violence, a moment of retribution. The hate and anger of years had been collecting in his soul now boiled up thanks to a moment of truth.

A silence fell about all three.

Warsh managed to sit. To work his back up using the stove. He took a bearing on his senses. He wiped at the blood running down his neck from the scalp wound.

"You don't think for a fuckin' moment," said Warsh, "I'd let you or anyone near a loaded gun when you're on that kind of rant."

Bill looked at the weapon. Fired it again, aiming the barrel straight up at the ceiling. There was that dead click of the hammer. Bill fired again, just to be sure. Same result.

"I know you too good, kid," said Warsh. "See... I'd a done what you did myself."

Warsh struggled to get up. He was dizzy. Viola got an arm around him.

"Right the table," she told Bill.

He did as Viola asked. She helped Warsh sit down.

Warsh swiped at the weapon which Bill still held.

"Consider this a lesson learned," Warsh said to his nephew. "See how easy it is for you to go Billy the Kid. Beware, boy."

Bill had it. He was upright now and walked out.

"Nothing to say!" Warsh shouted. "No further condemnations. You must be crowded with them condemnations. I know I am."

Viola had gone over to the sink and wet down a towel. She offered it to Warsh.

"Clean up the back of your head."

"Thanks," he said, taking the towel.

"I think you're gonna need stitches."

"I didn't know they were going to be on the train that day."

Viola looked out the kitchen doorway.

"But you did know what was going down on the train that day. And you didn't think to warn them... just in case?"

What he knew for all those years was his answer.

"No," he said. "I didn't. It was not the way we operated."

"Well," she said. "What does that say about you?"

"I got a word of advice...or a warning," said Warsh.

"Bring it on," said Viola.

"Burn everything...then forget it."

CHAPTER 202

Viola left Warsh alone with this new world reality.

The front door was open. She walked out onto the terrace. It had started to rain. Heavy drops that quickly left the street wet and slick.

She went downstairs. Bill was nowhere to be found. His car was there, his motorcycle was there. The neighborhood was dramatically still. She wandered out into the street, searching as she went.

Then she thought she saw something there in the tunnel, where the Esplanade tracks crossed over above Matthews Avenue.

A strange elusive figure, to be sure. Alone, smoking. A shadow touched by a bit of streetlamp.

She wondered what was going through his mind at that moment. Where this dark and precise act out in the kitchen would take him.

She went to him. Near the entrance to the tunnel she pressed up close beside him.

He touched her intimately, but he was far away.

"Where are you?" she said.

"I was thinking about my mother's wake. It was at Cooke's Funeral Home. Right by the elevated. You could hear the train above us going by, and I could see this crucifix on the wall above her casket tremor every time a train went past. Like some otherworldly reminder of what had gone down.

"But more than that, when it was time to close the casket and everyone to take their silent moment… When it was my turn I could not kiss my mother goodbye. I could not kiss her and I could not cry… like the others did.

"The woman lying there was not my mother. It was just a shell, a husk, a construct. What made my mother was gone."

He looked toward the house. The lights on the terrace stairs to Warsh's front door, which was still open.

"But Warsh... when it was his turn he could not stop crying. He could not cry enough. He kissed her again and again and again. He held her hand. He whispered to her. I wonder if he was already thinking about what he was involved in for the good of God and country that might have been responsible, at least in part, for her death. Did he ever imagine this night?"

She absorbed this heartbreaking confession as only one can who understands stolen love. And like that day in the blue Lincoln when she met the child Bill she kissed two fingers and touched them to the scar he had gotten just below his eye during his mother's murder.

They stood together with rain dropping from the eaves of the trestle and sure enough in time the lights of the subway cars and the rattle of the subway cars passed over them.

The earth tremored and the rain was all lit up and everything burned with urgency. And then everything turned quiet and still.

It was, she thought, like the passing of a life. But she did not express that to him.

"I crossed into enemy country tonight," said Bill. "Didn't I?"

"You sure did."

"What do you think?"

"It's not just what I think... it's what do we do with what I think."

BLOOD AND THUNDER SECRETS

CHAPTER 203

Malone was lunching down the street from his apartment at Chumley's Pub. He was eating alone and reading the *Times* when the maitre d' approached him with a house phone.

"Call for you, Mr. Malone."

He looked at the phone. Suffered a bellwether moment. Cursed privately because he knew. Then he put on his gentleman's voice.

"Malone, here."

It was the Costa woman alright, who said, "Have you decided on paying me… killing me… or possibly both?"

"I appreciate your humor. I have made the decision to proceed according to your request."

"Good. You'll have my directions set up for you later today, or early tomorrow."

"As you see fit. You know where to reach me."

"You're being very careful with your language," she said.

"Am I?"

"You know the saying… a word to the wise is sufficient."

"So they tell me," said Malone. "And I'm sure you follow that wisdom yourself. At least I hope so. Otherwise you would not have brought it up."

"Sincerely," she said. "By the way… I'll be working through a conduit."

Another layer of bad news, he thought, coming right at him.

"I see... And the conduit... Who might that be?"

"Viola Dash."

CHAPTER 204

Avalon was at Charlie's house. In the den, they talked. Charlie passed Avalon copies of two old New York State driver's licenses.

"The Costa woman... courtesy of the DMV."

Avalon looked the copies over.

"If Costa is her real name."

"This is the attorney's house on Bronxwood and Mace."

Charlie passed Avalon a snapshot of the place.

"By Saint Lucy's."

"Yeah."

The phone rang. Charlie answered. "It's Malone."

Charlie listened a minute or so then said, "Do you know who the conduit is?"

Charlie listened. The phone call lasted only a bit longer, then Charlie hung up.

"Fuck," he said.

"What?"

"There's gonna be a conduit involved in this."

"But the same rules apply," said Avalon.

"Do you know who the conduit is?"

"No."

"But I deal with the Costa woman first?"

"You deal with the Costa woman first."

"Do you know when it's to happen?"

"We're to get word sometime between late today and tomorrow."

"Nothing like keeping it tight."

"It's the Costa woman… she's a street pro."

A car pulled into the driveway. Charlie got up and looked out the blinds.

"Perfect timing," he said, "is always anything but."

"What," said Avalon.

"It's my daughter."

"You want me to—"

Avalon pointed to the door.

"No," said Charlie. "Just keep it low key."

"I can do low key."

"She and I are in a bad place."

CHAPTER 205

Viola crossed the living room as her father appeared at the French doors to the patio.

"I didn't exactly expect you back," he said.

"I have more stuff I need to pick up."

"You're moving out… entirely?"

"The verdict is still in doubt on that."

"Got it," he said.

She saw someone on the patio through the French doors. It was Avalon. He was smoking.

"Who is that?" said Viola. "I think I know him."

"No… You don't know him."

"I do… I've seen him before."

Avalon saw he was being stared at and talked about, it seemed, so he cordially saluted Viola.

"Charming," she said, in a way that could have different meanings.

"What have you been doing," said Viola's father, "plotting the overthrow of the world?"

"I thought that was your department."

"Very sharp... and very quick."

He looked like he had wanted to say something more personal, more human, giving. But he was caught flathearted and came up short.

Viola's private phone rang and she hustled to the kitchen to answer it. Charlie watched her. She spent the whole phone call listening and then hung up and rejoined her father.

"I'll have to come back later and finish up... if that's alright."

"It's still your home."

She felt the awkward moment that followed much like her father did. Maybe more so. He looked taken down in some way.

"Is it something important... the phone call?"

"It's not something I can talk about," she said.

He nodded. He understood.

"Good luck," he said. "Be careful... and cautious."

She wanted to kiss him on the cheek before she left, but she did not. Once in the car, once out the driveway, once heading down that heavily treed street with all those well to do homes that had been part of the childhood there that escaped her, she began to cry. It was the time, and it wasn't the time, for such things.

CHAPTER 206

Viola was looking down at Malone's desk where a copy of her personal ad and those articles connected to it in the Bronx newspapers were laid out.

"This was your idea."

"Yes, sir."

"You might say it was prescient in what it exposed."

"You also might say, sir, it was pure luck."

He nodded. There were snapshots taken from the rally…turned minor riot, also on the desk, which he began to thumb through.

"You handled yourself well at the rally… People will trust you as an honest player. I trust you."

He folded his hands and sat there like the quintessential corporate officer.

"The actions taken by Blue and Baum and those connected to the drug operations during those years were ill advised and illegal. The program is no longer in operation and the truth will come out eventually. And I hope people like yourself will be instrumental in exposing that truth. Would you like to be part of that?"

"I would, sir, yes."

CHAPTER 207

Costa made her call from a phone booth in Grand Central Station. As she dialed Costa stared at her next self reflected in the glass. Courtesy of the wallets she'd lifted she'd treated herself to a cheapo Vidal Sassoon haircut and then did a bleach job on it. She bought herself some clothes in a secondhand shop in the Village and topped off this new look with a funky newsboy cap.

She knew in the end they would come after her. That they were not just gonna let her walk—no such luck.

Gardner answered the call.

"Put Viola on," said Costa.

She could hear Gardner say, "It's Beonca Costa." And then Viola was on the line.

"It's Viola."

"You don't have to speak. Just listen. If you recall where we met that first time, meet me there tomorrow. You may have to wait the whole day. You may be followed. I assume you will. Be wary. If you're so inclined, carry a gun. If you're cool with this, just hang up."

CHAPTER 208

When she hung up, Viola looked around Gardner's office. As usual, Gardner was there behind his desk. As for Bill, he was across the room in that large chair that seemed to have become a second home.

"That was short," said Bill.

"Very," said Viola.

"What did she say?" Gardner wondered.

"That I should consider carrying a gun."

"Thoughtful soul," said Gardner.

"Where are you two to meet?" said Bill.

"Where we met before."

"Got it," said Bill.

Gardner was staring at a sealed envelope on his desk.

In it was a detailed account by Beonca Costa of certain actions taken by named parties—some that were conveniently, or not so conveniently, deceased—who had been working in direct coordination with governmental agencies. And some that were outside that world. Actions that dated back to the mid 1950s, right up to the Lake George Murders.

The letter was to be signed and notarized by Costa, at the appropriate moment in time. And that moment was when the money she asked for was in hand.

"It's a death warrant," said Bill.

Gardner looked up. Bill was standing at the desk, pointing at the envelope with its draft of Costa's account.

"Warsh… Viola's father… Death warrant. Beyond what we know and could validate."

Bill looked over at Viola. That seedling moment putting an ad into the Bronx newspapers led to this, and where that would lead to—

"I've killed them both," said Viola. "And who knows who else."

They all knew, but left it unsaid.

CHAPTER 209

Gardner initiated the next call.

When the phone was answered Gardner said, "We're ready here… She set it for tomorrow, or the latest the day after… For her safety, what do you think?"

Gardner hung up.

"Malone?" said Bill.

"Malone," said Gardner, who followed that with "His person is on the way. Viola knows him, so says Malone."

Gardner addressed Viola. "Malone is adamant. Anyone but him arrives, abandon the plan and protect yourselves."

Bill went over to Viola. She looked uncertain.

"Are we doing the right thing?" she said.

Bill had something else on his mind.

"Who is the one coming?" said Bill.

"I think it's that Rick guy."

"Is he a fool?" said Bill. "Someone who is being used... Or something else?"

Viola shrugged. Was overwhelmed. Went back to "Are we doing the right thing?"

"How do you define doing the right thing?" said Bill.

"We could dump everything over to some authority... couldn't we?" She looked to Gardner for an answer. "Tell us something."

"Everything we know rests on a statement by Beonca Costa. What do you think would be her response to such a suggestion?"

Viola went and sat. She rested her arms on her legs. Her cheeks were flushed, and that eerie stillness was coming back, as if the world were waiting on something terrible.

"Do you think Warsh and my father know what's going down?"

"I can't answer that," said Bill.

"Are they part of it?"

Bill knew what that meant. If they were part of it, what would be the verdict when it came to their own children?

CHAPTER 210

Warsh might as well have been told he was going to die.

They had been following Avalon and that graduate student who was into the cause. Warsh in the shotgun seat, Charlie driving that weighty Lincoln of his, keeping it at a safe distance so the kid did not catch on. But as soon as they turned off Pelham Parkway and onto

Eastchester Road, Warsh knew. Rick's destination was Bronxwood and Mace.

Warsh made a hellish sound and cursed out Charlie.

"You didn't say one single word about this," said Warsh.

"Damn right."

"Who's the conduit… The carrier… Your daughter… My nephew?"

"Viola… Billy the Kid… Does it matter? Think of them as a package deal."

"That's not funny. You're delivering all of us into the teeth of a disaster."

"Who fucked up at Lake George… That night led to this… But, hey… shit like this happens in the best of families."

Charlie was cold and crass and decidedly ugly and Warsh had a rush of hatred for that fuck shit sitting there that he'd partnered with for years. Through a procession of clandestine acts, conquests and calamities, blood and thunder secrets, and more secrets, even a war where they both survived with medals earned. And now—

"I see the way you're staring at me," said Charlie.

"No… you can't see how I'm staring at you in here."

And by "in here," Warsh meant his heart, which he was beating against with a fist.

"Malone was close to having you put down over Lake George, okay," said Charlie. "That's what the priest from Laos's demise was all about. To see if you'd hold up or crack out. And then what do I do about it."

"What about Bill and Viola?"

"Maybe you'll come up with a brilliant move before we have to clock out."

"Who's the conduit?"

"My daughter, I suspect."

CHAPTER 211

The shades had been closed so no one could look into the house. Bill sat beside Viola. He held her hand in his and in the other rested his handgun. When there came this sudden knock at the door, everyone jumped at the sound.

Viola peeked through the blinds from the dark.

"It's him," said Viola.

"You're sure?"

"Very sure."

Gardner got up. He waited until Bill and Viola had softly gone up the stairs and into the dark as they'd planned.

When Gardner opened the door he was greeted by a young Puerto Rican graduate student carrying a small backpack.

"Come in," said Gardner.

"You Gardner?"

"I'm Gardner... And you're Rick. I'll relieve you now from that responsibility," said Gardner, reaching for the backpack.

Rick pulled it out of Gardner's reach. He looked around. "Where's Viola?"

"She's not here."

"I need to talk to her before I hand this over."

"That was not told to me."

Gardner stepped forward, Rick stepped back.

"I need to talk to her... And I know she's here."

He called out into the darkened house.

"Viola... Can you hear me? I need to talk to you for one minute... Just a minute."

Gardner wasn't having it. He went straight for the phone. "I'm going to call Mr. Malone and you can have this out with him."

As he started dialing, Rick was right there. "Please…."

CHAPTER 212

Rick pulled the receiver so hard its connection tore loose. "It's important… Please." Rick didn't wait. He took off down the hallway calling to Viola. Shouting. Then there in the shadow of the second floor stairway he thought he saw the slightest movement and up he went. His voice piercing the quiet.

"Remember me talking to you at the rally."

Something rammed into him. Something was now pressed against his throat.

It was Bill, and it was a handgun.

Rick put his hands in the air.

"I'm not a threat."

"Put the gun down, Bill," said Viola.

Bill put it down. Mostly because Viola asked him.

"Here… take this." Rick handed the backpack to Bill. "This will show you… I'm not a threat."

"Bring the backpack to Gardner, will you, Bill… Don't make the call," she shouted. "Hear me?" Gardner answered that he heard her. "Leave Rick and I here, will you, Bill?"

Bill hesitated, but before he did leave, he took one last moment and pressed the barrel of his handgun to Rick's chest.

"You're telling me where the hole is gonna be," said Rick. "Very cinematic."

Bill's answer was to take the backpack downstairs and let Gardner do his thing.

Now it was Rick and Viola.

"I know there's money in that backpack. A lot of money. And I'm telling you... Dump this whole thing. Whatever it is... Split... Walk... Sprint... There's something fucked going down here. There's bad things moving around that money. I didn't realize how bad until tonight."

He took her by the shoulders in the dark of the second floor landing, a prison of shadows unto itself. "I thought America was going after a great thing. I thought I could be part of it. But this? I don't know... Have I been fooled? Have I?"

He shook Viola. "Do you know?"

CHAPTER 213

Before they were over and done with Rick, Bill had slipped out of the house, taking the stairwell from the terrace over the dining room, down into the side yard. He was lying in wait to see whether Rick had come alone.

He had not.

When Bill hustled back inside, Viola and Gardner were in the den standing at the desk where the money for Costa was all laid out.

"He was driven here," said Bill. "He ran down the block and got into a Buick Invicta... maroon. With borrowed plates, I bet."

Bill got his first real look at the money.

"Pack this up and let's get to Jersey... There's no telling who else is out there."

He had been talking and didn't notice how conspiratorially quiet the two were.

"Something is happening here... What?"

"What if we don't bring her the money?" said Viola.

CHAPTER 214

"You got any feeling the Costa woman is in there," said Warsh. "And all this is just—"

"Decoration?" said Charlie. "I do not."

He'd parked his Lincoln far enough down the street so as not to be seen.

Warsh glanced at his watch. "It's been almost an hour since that kid—"

"It may take longer. All night, maybe. We're not paid by the hour."

"Gardner is a smart attorney. He might have the woman in there."

"Another woman… maybe. But she's a hyper bitch. A lifetime scammer. Look at how she operates. She wouldn't let herself be cornered in. What's with you? None of this is new."

"No?" said Warsh.

Charlie realized, "Yeah, yeah… You're right."

"Hey," said Warsh. He pointed.

What they could see through that long stretch of shadows, two people at least had come out of the dark house and were making for the driveway.

When the doors of the car in the driveway opened, it was pretty clear. Bill and Viola got in. Gardner went back to the house, giving the two kids a thumbs up on the way.

Charlie turned on the Lincoln.

Warsh saw Bill was behind the wheel as the kid did a swift turn up Mace.

"That's a car of mine," said Warsh. "One I'm tricking out. The car is fuckin' regged to me."

"Billy the Kid is making sure no one gets out of this in one piece. Let alone alive."

CHAPTER 215

Viola was in the shotgun seat, snaked around, squinting to see better out the back window and through the flow of headlights following, for anyone or anything that might signal bad news.

When she sees what she thinks she sees, out of her mouth comes a furious run of invective.

"What?" says Bill.

"A Lincoln."

"Where?"

"Three cars back."

He maneuvered the rearview.

"I don't see it."

"Make a turn... any turn."

They were up where US 1 crossed Mace and he sped through the open and wide intersection and took a hard left and sure enough, the Lincoln made the same hard left.

Viola was furious and frightened. "It's my father back there, alright. That's his Lincoln...." Her voice was venomous. "Everything about us is this country... Everything... Everything."

"Forget it," said Bill.

"First it's being put down... then shut down...."

Bill made a radical turn, the Lincoln made the same radical turn. Bill crossed over the dividing line to pass a truck and the Lincoln followed suit.

"Put down… shut down… and now run down. Fuck him. Fuck Warsh. He's back there too."

The next turn Bill's car was almost taken out by a bus. The car swerved momentarily out of control and that big old heavy Lincoln did no better, skipping up onto the curb and then slamming back down on the pavement.

CHAPTER 216

"You want to kill us both?" said Warsh. "And them?"

Charlie sped through a red light.

"That answer enough," said Charlie. "We get the woman, the money can't be far away. We have the money, the woman will be close behind."

Bill's car kept picking up speed, as if in sheer defiance at being chased down.

"Maybe we can convince them," said Warsh.

"Convince them? Do they look like they're in the market to be convinced… or persuaded? Threatened, maybe… Maybe."

They were kicking it across town.

"Where the fuck are they going?" said Warsh.

"I'm gonna stop them," said Charlie, "if I have to run them off the road."

Warsh braced himself against the dashboard.

"Suppose we stop them," said Warsh. "But they don't give up the woman or the money. What then?"

"There is no answer… except one."

"We can't go there."

"If they even think they're gonna die," said Charlie, "maybe they cave."

"It can't go there."

"Can't go there," said Charlie. "Can't go there... Brother, we are there... Look."

CHAPTER 217

They were burning it down Webster making for the bridge. Bill had turned into a block of dead warehouses, all brick and iron and filthy gutters. And he'd come to a dead stop and was getting out of his car and striding straight for the Lincoln, gun in hand, while Viola had slipped over into the driver's seat.

The Lincoln came to an ugly stop... God knows. A bare sketch of lights, the block all dark and black and the Lincoln... well, Warsh yelled out, "The kid's got a gun," and there was smoke from the brakes fuming off the tires like nothing you could imagine.

THE ASSASSINATION OF A CULTURE

CHAPTER 218

As he got out of the Lincoln, Warsh shouted, "Put that gun away!"

"He's not gonna put it away!" Charlie screamed. "You're gonna have to take it away from him!"

"No chance of that," said Bill. "Not him, not you."

Bill kept on coming.

"There's so much serious shit happening here you can't realize," said Warsh. "The woman… we got to have her."

Viola shouted from the car, "You and my father both! You know what you are… The assassination of a culture… that's what!"

"We're done with you," said Bill. "You're not gonna ghost us."

Bill was sure not putting the gun away. He was closing in on the Lincoln. On both men. But he was wary enough. He saw Charlie move toward the glove compartment.

"Don't do it, Charlie."

"The kid has lost his mind threatening us like this… you hear me, Warsh?"

"Not lost it… Got it under control," said Bill.

He got close enough now to the two men. He aimed the weapon at Warsh.

"The gun is loaded, Papi."

Bill fired. He fired right past Warsh. Bill had fired at a rear tire on the Lincoln. The tire blew out, blew completely out. It made a nasty hissing sound.

Then Bill closed in on a front tire.

Charlie was apoplectic. He stormed out of the car. He was wielding a crowbar he'd pulled out from under his seat.

Too late.

Bill had already taken aim.

Charlie threw the crowbar at Bill, but missed him. It went clanging across the asphalt.

There were two tires now making nasty hissing noises.

"Your night is done!" yelled Viola. "Let's get out of here, Bill."

Charlie was coming at Bill like a bull, but Bill got out of the way and brought his handgun down on top of Charlie's skull.

Charlie hit the pavement. He made a sound that only bordered on something human.

Bill ran back to his car.

"We got to have the woman… And the money." Warsh kept on with this demand, pointless as it was.

But Charlie, he was on his knees now, shaking a fist. "I'll kill you for this."

CHAPTER 219

They lay together in the Bergen Mall outdoor parking lot in the back seat of Bill's car. The moon a singular presence over the back window, marking the time till dawn and so deal with what was, and what was to come.

They made love and not just for the pure passion it afforded, but to fight off all the travesties of life that surrounded them as best they could.

"I feel like we're being chased down by our own history," whispered Viola, "as if someone, somewhere, could hear. Someone with the power to threaten. And our history, everything about us, that is us, is linked to this other history. A history I do not understand, do not fathom, but is there, has a life all its own, separate from us. And it moves in shadows. And it means to outwit and overwhelm us. To break us…."

She paused, caught up in her own thoughts. "What do you think?" she said.

He lay there with his hands behind his head, looking up into the back window mural of a black night sky, getting a feel for all she'd said.

"I think we might be better at drawing blood than you realize."

CHAPTER 220

Mass was almost over when Viola arrived at the chapel in the Bergen Mall. Bill waited out in the hallway. He could see through the glass walling the Costa woman sitting alone a few rows back of the handful of parishioners. She was the redecorated Beonca Costa.

Costa straightened up when Viola walked in and sat beside her. There was the flush of excitement on the woman's face.

"I see you touched up," said Viola.

"Look different… feel different… be different."

Viola nodded. She was about to drop the hammer.

"I prayed for this moment," said Beonca.

"Stop praying," said Viola. "Because that prayer is not gonna be answered… We're not gonna pay you."

CHAPTER 221

Viola had walked out, Costa hot on her heels. Neither wanted some drama to be played out in the chapel. Too many sets of inquiring eyes.

When they started up the hallway Costa couldn't get the words out fast enough.

"I've been praying my guts out… Living in fear… I think I'm free and you drop this on me… Now… Here… Why? You going to keep the money?"

"It's going back."

Beonca grabbed Viola by the arm, and hard. "Give it back!"

Bill was up the hallway. Beonca saw him just as he started to come toward them.

"You?" said Beonca.

"Me," said Bill.

Bill quietly got Viola loose of the Costa woman's grasp.

"You strip me on my money, so I come down hard on them. I threaten with that document we all put together."

"That's the idea," said Bill.

"Go to the authorities," said Viola. "Tell your story… Go to the newspapers… the *Times*… Tell your story… Show them the document."

"You want to drive us all out into the open," said Costa. "Did you have this in the works the whole time? Are you that clever… That crazy?"

Beonca looked from one to the other to try to discover some answer in their expressions. Some tell she could latch onto. But she came up empty. They'd given her nothing to work with, nothing to hustle them with, to convince them with, to plead with.

"Remember this," said Beonca. "If they can find me, they'll kill me. You don't need to be found to be killed… because they already have."

"You know," said Bill, "we still have no idea of how much you told us is actually true… and how much truth you left out."

"Ask your fuckin' uncle, or father, or whatever he is. I told you the truth… And I know it."

The Costa woman started away.

"You haven't heard me plead, or beg, or play on your sympathies, and you won't. I won't even threaten to kill you myself one day."

CHAPTER 222

Avalon was at Rick's apartment. He was waiting on a call from Malone. A contingency call would be closer to it. He and the college boy played gin while the three women had only begun to stir, since they worked night shifts.

The call eventually came. It was Malone alright. Avalon took it. Rick got up and went and poured himself a little more coffee.

Malone told Avalon he'd just received word from the Costa woman. She was in a state of panic… and rage. Viola Dash had not come across with the money, and wasn't going to.

When Avalon asked about Charlie and Warsh the answer was pure disconnect. It seems Billy the Kid had shot the Lincoln's wheels right out from under them. Left the two of them on the west side of the Bronx to walk.

Avalon had a hard time believing the Dash kid and the Wild One pulled off a mind blower like that.

Avalon glanced at Rick, sipping away.

Avalon put on a faux smile while he wondered—what this nothing Puerto Rican might know. Was he in on any phase of it.

Malone was telling Avalon that the Dash girl was pressing Costa to go public with her information as a means of keeping herself alive. No chance of that, if you heard Costa. But this whole situation was drowning in bad options.

"You need a plan, chief," said Avalon.

You know what Malone told him. That as of right now, this moment… Avalon was the plan.

CHAPTER 223

As they came back from Jersey, Viola suggested they check in on Rick. They stopped at a diner and called him from a payphone, but the line was busy. They decided to swing over to his apartment and ate while they drove.

It was a hot day, a noisy day. The building hallway was woefully dark, just like the other day. And it smelled of greasy food, just like the other day.

Viola knocked on the door, but oddly enough, it wasn't closed, and it just eased open some.

She looked at Bill. After last night nothing was for certain anymore.

"Call to him," said Bill quietly.

Viola leaned into the opening and called to Rick. The only sound from the apartment was the television.

"The mother is bedridden… MS," she said. "Maybe everyone else is out."

Bill moved Viola aside a bit. Then, using his forearm, he pushed the door open enough they could both slide in and leave no fingerprints. Once in Bill used his forearm again to get the door back as it was.

They stood in the atrium and Viola called out once again, but to no avail.

She took a few steps into the living room, while Bill started for the kitchen and back hallway. He saw something and pointed.

There was a shadow of a person sitting in a high backed chair facing the television. Viola nodded and thinking it might be the mother came on and bent over the armrest and that's when Bill saw Viola reel and almost tumble back over herself.

One of the aunts sat in that chair, her head in a plastic bag that was tightened around with tape.

The woman's eyes were open, her flesh blue. She was the worst kind of dead.

But there was more.

Bill was snapping his fingers. Viola came over and stopped in the doorway.

It was a gruesome scene before her. Fliers from the rally were scattered all over the linoleum. There were slipshod stacks on the table. They were spotted with blood.

Rick sat in a kitchen table chair slumped over. He had been shot in the side of the head.

Bill was in the kitchen by the body. He was looking down at the table. He motioned for Viola to come over. This she did not want to do, but did.

Bill had been pointing at one of the fliers on the table. It had been turned over. Beside the blood on the back, there was writing on it… *Forgive me…* and then Rick had signed his name.

"Look there," said Viola.

On the floor, just under Rick's chair… a handgun.

CHAPTER 224

"There's a young man asking to see you."

Malone looked up at his assistant. "Is his name Warsh?"

"Yes, sir."

"Usher him in… If you hear shouting or gunshots, just disregard them."

"Excuse me, sir?"

"Never mind."

Malone got up from his desk and went over to the window. He looked out on the chance something was there that needed seeing.

The office door opened and there he was.

"Mr. Malone," said Bill.

Bill was carrying the same backpack Rick had the night before.

"I was told by Gardner that this was yours, and should be returned."

"If it isn't Billy the Kid... or at least that's what Charlie Dash calls you."

"Fuck Charlie Dash."

Bill set the backpack on Malone's desk.

Malone glanced out the window one last time. Then he said, "You uncle never mentioned how political you were."

"Politics is not my thing."

"Then what do you think all this is?"

Malone pointed at the backpack, but his inference was much more broad.

"When I was put away in juvenile detention we'd have to suffer through endless lectures on the right way to live. In those five years one thing I remembered... *It's more important to your future that you are honest in the present.* I never really took it to heart... except now."

Malone nodded. Took one quick glance out the window as he started back to his desk.

"She's not out there," said Bill.

"She?"

"You know damn well who I mean."

Bill started out. Malone spoke as he did. "You weren't up in Spanish Harlem by any chance?"

Bill stopped at the door.

"How 'bout you?"

CHAPTER 225

There was a crime up in Spanish Harlem waiting to be discovered.

As their attorney of record, Gardner listened to everything Bill and Viola told him. Every detail of what they knew, had seen, had done.

While all three talked about what came next, headlights pulled into the driveway.

Bill looked out the window.

"It's a Lincoln," he said, "with two new tires."

"What shall we do?" said Viola.

"Listen… no more," said Gardner.

Bill let Charlie Dash in. He looked Bill over. He looked his daughter over. Nothing good there.

Charlie turned his attention to Gardner. "I need to talk to you… alone."

"You kids go make yourself comfortable," said Gardner.

"Yeah," said Charlie. "Go relax before the bloodletting."

They left the office for the kitchen. Doors were closed, appropriately so.

"You know why I'm here," said Charlie.

"You're a dead end."

"Convince them to see this through, otherwise… they'll be broken… Or worse."

"That's your daughter you're talking about."

"What she did will see Warsh and me killed… So, I'm on the dark side of the road. But… I can blow her up right now… him too."

Gardner's voice rose. "We had this conversation twenty years ago. As a matter of fact we had it more recently... remember? You fuck with those kids on this one thing I see you wiped off the map. I see the cruel politics of life suck out your blood. And give you untold suffering. Am I freaking you out... Find someone else to work your deal with the woman."

"Costa is afraid what we'll do to her."

"And she should be. She's not a street fool. That's why she picked your daughter to be her conduit."

The argument went on for a bad half hour, until their very voices got worn out. It ended with the slamming of a door and headlights sweeping out of the driveway.

CHAPTER 226

They could hear the argument echoing up through the floorboards like ghosts out of the past.

"What do you think it was all about, down there?"

"No idea."

"Not even a guess?"

"It goes back twenty years," said Bill. "You heard them. What would I know about something that goes back twenty years... that they don't want me to know?"

"Do you ever hear Gardner make a threat like that?" said Viola.

"I never heard him make a threat... period. But whatever it is—"

"Do you think he'd tell us, if we ask him?"

"You hear him down there."

"I mean we come on hard."

"He's running interference. He doesn't want us to know. You heard... they fought recently about this."

"And why does my father want to use it against us… I wonder if Warsh knows. And why isn't he here?"

"That struck me too."

"This freaks me out," said Viola.

"You mean 'cause it affects us somehow… like a threat."

"I mean it might be about us… Or one of us."

CHAPTER 227

They came downstairs once Gardner was alone. He sat at his desk facing a cocktail. He was tied up in knots. They stood in the doorway waiting to be spoken to, or at least acknowledged.

Gardner finally said, "I don't think I can stop the inevitable."

That was it.

Viola then said, "Is there anything else you're okay with telling us?"

"Find a new life for yourselves. You can effect change anywhere."

They walked to Bill's car as if they had just been given the time and date for the end of the world.

In the car Viola put a hand on Bill's as he went to turn on the ignition.

"You heard him," she said. "We can make a new life somewhere… effect change anywhere!"

"But not here."

"Isn't that just like you to tell me the truth."

She'd said this with affection. He leaned over and kissed her. They seemed more mature than their years. The proximity of death will sometimes do that for you.

"Wait for a minute," he said. He left the keys in the ignition so she could let the radio play.

Bill went back inside. Gardner was holding a small framed photograph that Bill knew well. Gardner held it up for a moment.

"The forgotten days."

Bill nodded.

"I believe I know what you're going to say," said Gardner.

"I wouldn't be surprised."

"I know that you're capable, son."

A moment passed filled with foreboding.

"They'll be at Charlie's house tonight," said Gardner. "They'll talk this through, then call me. Give me one more good old fashioned threat to pass onto you."

Bill nodded.

"If anything should happen to—"

"Don't even say it, son. I'm miles ahead of you."

CHAPTER 228

They drove to Bill's place. Night was closing in. Bill watched the express along the Esplanade. A chapter in his life in long, deep shadows and chopped light.

Viola was getting ready to take a shower.

Bill suggested she hike over to Gardner's and he would catch up with her there a little later.

She didn't bother him with questions like "What's up?" or "Where you goin'?" You see, she knew she would not get the truth.

She had a fix on the details he was leaving out, and she knew if you're going to give it all to a person, you give it all. Fuck shortcuts, fuck compromises.

There are no words suitable or fitting at times like that... There are just the long deep shadows and coffins of light from the train on the Esplanade, and the sound of its steeled fury.

Then Bill was gone, and she was in the shower trying to wash off the death they'd witnessed.

CHAPTER 229

There were three men at the Dash home that night. Charlie Dash, of course, also Warsh, and finally the young man they called Avalon.

They were in the sprawling family room in the midst of a contentious debate on how to proceed. Dash and Warsh had to make the decision to go ahead. Avalon would create and carry out the plan.

Warsh was emotionally in over his head at this point and was trying to argue around the bleak reality that was before them.

Yet a plan would be created, and it would go forward, with Warsh or without. Dash was better at separating realities—the reality being these were their children they were discussing.

In a moment of absolute frustration Charlie took the phone, walked to where Warsh was sitting, and slammed it down on the table.

"Gardner is expecting our call… Put the fear of God in him."

"They don't believe we'll take the next step," said Avalon. "Until we take the next step."

"Then it's all gone," said Warsh. "Our lives—"

He looked at Charlie. Warsh saw he'd made his decision. He'd crossed the white line. Now it was the doing.

"Maybe we don't make the call," said Warsh. "We do nothing. Let them sweat it out for a few more days while we work on the

Costa woman. Try to find another conduit she can trust."

"It's you who wants a few days," said Charlie.

Avalon slapped his hands together and pointed toward the television at the far end of the room.

WPIX News. The bodies up in Spanish Harlem had finally been discovered. The three men crowded around the screen. The newscaster was calling it a murder and not a murder and suicide.

"Maybe this will put the fear of God in them," said Avalon.

Then, moments later, with one grief delivered there on the television screen and one grief yet to come, the lights in the whole house went out.

CHAPTER 230

"Fuck it... fuse box," said Charlie. "Hang here and I'll take care of it."

Charlie made his way to the back of the house. The fuse box was on the wall beside the garage. Charlie had to pass the back stairwell from the kitchen up to the second floor. And what does he see in the shadows blocking the door?

A shot rang out.

Charlie was hit in the thigh, right beneath the hip. The bone shattered. He was driven backwards. He heard Warsh and Avalon calling out to him. His meaty frame dropped under its own weight. He was calling back to the others, shouting and ripped with pain. "It's your fuckin' kid, Warsh... He's in the house!"

Charlie was trying to lift himself, holding on to the stair railing. The next shot caught him in a pouch of back flesh and blood blew all over the wall.

He grimaced so hard it near brought him to tears. He wasn't getting up anymore. He had a pistol in his waistband, as always. Little good it did him. He could hardly get it loose, tucked as it was under his belly.

CHAPTER 231

Warsh knew the house. But it didn't take much to find Charlie. Just follow his agony.

Warsh and Avalon bent over the dying man. Avalon kept watch as Warsh looked his partner over.

"He's bleeding to death," said Warsh.

"Got a gun?"

"Maybe," said Warsh, who knew Charlie always had one tucked inside his waistband.

He wriggled an arm under Charlie's belly. He found the gun after some searching and Charlie crying out at the pain that went with it.

Warsh checked the gun.

Charlie's breathing was faulty.

"It was Bill who did this… Do you hear?"

"I hear, Charlie," said Warsh.

A lifetime was on the clock. More than one, really. The kid had come to fight and a man you've spent it all with was gasping himself to death.

It's hideous to get what you deserve.

"We got to make sure," whispered Avalon, "your kid doesn't get out of here."

Warsh looked up at Avalon as if he were a fool.

"The kid isn't about getting out of the house."

"What then?" said Avalon.

"He means to make sure *we* don't get out of the house."

CHAPTER 232

"That's a course correction," whispered Avalon, "that I can live with."

Warsh checked how many shots the handgun had in it.

Something coursed across the room behind them. Something shattered against a wall. Something that sounded like glass, and something metallic caroming across the floor.

Avalon fired. Shots were returned.

Then there was a fierce volley after that, spiked with bursts of light. The rooms quickly clouded. There was very little sound, and suddenly no movement. It was just a dark corridor of rooms connecting.

Warsh was sitting on the floor with his back against the wall at the edge of an alcove. He tried to move, but his legs would not obey.

"Avalon," he whispered. "Avalon... I'm hit."

Avalon did not answer.

"Bill... did you hear me... I'm hit."

Bill did not answer.

Warsh closed his eyes for a moment. Live life wasted, die life wasted. He had been speaking to the darkness. His answer came a moment later. Someone moved quickly across the open space. The briefest outline against the glittery moonlight on a French door.

Then more graying smoke. And a light cutting through all that floating haze, panning the darkness until it came upon Avalon's dead body, the arms splayed.

CHAPTER 233

The light again began its search.

Bill stepped over Avalon's body.

"I'm here," said Warsh. "By the alcove."

The light swept the scene and then it found him, there like something captured. Some blood pooling around his lower back.

"I can't move my legs," he said.

The light kept closing in until Warsh could see the boy turned man behind the light.

Bill knelt down. Saw Warsh still had his gun. He took it from Warsh with one gloved hand and tossed it aside.

"Did I kill Avalon… or did you?"

"Does it matter?" said Warsh.

"No."

Bill used the light to look over the wound, Warsh noticed the gun in Bill's other hand.

"Recognize it?" said Bill.

"I do," said Warsh.

"That was a terrible thing done up in Spanish Harlem."

"He was a fuckin' communist," said Warsh. "Here to subvert order, cause chaos. The riot you were in… bought and paid for. He wasn't about voting rights. Two of the women he lived with were agents from Cuba. Viola was a rabbit to draw them out."

While he talked Bill stood and using the light made his way to the living room phone.

He came back with the phone on a long cable. He knelt and set it on the floor beside Warsh.

Bill then took the gun from the Spanish Harlem killing which he held in his other gloved hand and pressed it into Warsh's palm, forcing him to take it.

"You got choices," said Bill. "You can call the paramedics and take your chances... You can shoot yourself."

Bill stood.

"You can even shoot me first," said Bill.

They both took one last measure of each other's lives... and souls.

"Goodbye, Uncle."

CHAPTER 234

Bill's return to Gardner's house was prefaced by a hoarse motorcycle engine and a lone headlight flaring past Saint Lucy's Grotto then slanting hard into the Bronxwood driveway.

The front door was open and Viola in the hallway waiting by the time he came up the walk. What Viola saw in his face brought such pain to her very being. He had been crying. The tears leaving grime stains down his cheeks. She hid her emotions behind her affection because sometimes that is one's only place to contend with what is.

In the hallway he put an arm around her, and she did the same to him.

"You'll never walk alone with this," she said in a hushed way.

Bill entered the office and there Gardner sat at his desk. As Bill walked to the bar, he said, "You know... I'm not sure I'd recognize you away from that desk."

Bill slid a glass across the bartop. He reached for a bottle without even looking at what it was. He went to pour a drink but his hand was trembling so he could not and it was left to Viola.

Bill looked over at Gardner, who sat there smoking. He was quiet. His forever good looks were haggard that night, over what had been, and what he was going to tell Bill about what now was.

"Let's get on with it," said Bill.

Gardner nodded, then obliged. "I received a call… There's been killings at the Dash house… Charlie among the victims… It seems Warsh was involved in the murders of Charlie and another man… He gave his confession over the phone… He then committed suicide."

Gardner drew on his cigarette. Paused a bit, as much for himself and Viola as for the youth. "Tomorrow," he said, "we all have been requested to go in for identification purposes, first and foremost. Then they'll tell us whatever they can… and question us regarding what we might be able to add to the investigation."

Bill stood there, exhausted. He nodded. He then started for the door.

"I'm going to crash upstairs, if you don't mind," said Bill.

At the door Gardner had one last detail to be dealt with.

"In the morning," said Gardner, "we'll need to organize our stories. What we share… what we don't."

CHAPTER 235

Bill and Viola lay in bed, in the dark, the radio playing. They were side by side in one of those classic couple tropes.

She wanted to ask if her father had suffered, but of course she didn't. She just filed her question away in the back of her mind, where grief goes to bide its time.

"Where's it all going?" said Bill. "That's all I was thinking on the way back here. And I mean… our whole world story."

"One foot in glory... one in the grave," said Viola. "That kind of thing?"

They lay quietly with the question through a couple of songs, and the usual run of commercials totally out of touch with the moment.

She'd been thinking about what he'd asked and she had seen something that caught her eye and she wanted to lay it on him.

It was the day of the rally. She had been up on 116th Street. There was an old building, a tired looking thing, three stories of brick and all boarded up. A former apartment, with businesses on the ground floor.

It had been a nice place, once upon a time. You could see that. The detail work, the window trim. All very nice. But the building now was covered with graffiti, especially political and social graffiti.

Graffiti marking the times—the assassination of a president—the escalation of a far away war—voting rights—equality for all—the murder of a black leader—and, of course, the standard vile epithets that slay the mind.

A recent addition to that statement mural, across the front wall, in bold letters—*America v. America... Outcome Uncertain.*

Viola had lifted herself so she could see Bill better in the dark.

She had taken a snapshot of the building that day. A couple of them, in fact. She handed one to Bill. He looked it over.

"Get what it's saying," said Viola.

CHAPTER 236

The next morning, Bill drove them all downtown. By then they had organized their stories.

Their first destination was the coroner, for identification purposes. The next would be the Bronx division headquarters, for questioning about the crime and what, if anything, homicide could learn from the families that might further the investigation as to why the murder happened. Even though they ostensibly had a confession from Warsh.

The day was warm and clear and perfect for anything but what was before them. It was a quiet ride. The radio wasn't even on.

Gardner was riding shotgun. Viola was coiled up in the back. Gardner looked from one to the other. Bill was smoking a Kool to try and cut some of that anxiety off at the pass. Viola seemed intent on a snapshot of some kind.

To kill the silence some, Gardner said, "What are you looking at back there?"

It would turn out to be one of the snapshots Viola had taken of the building on 116th Street.

Bill glanced at Viola. "America v. America," he said.

And Viola answered, "Outcome uncertain."

"I don't get it," said Gardner.

"Show him," said Bill.

At a stoplight Viola leaned forward and passed the photo to Gardner.

"I took it the day of the rally," said Viola. "See what some thought jockey painted there in all that graffiti."

CHAPTER 237

Gardner took the photo in hand. Checked it out.

America v. America... Outcome Uncertain.

Gardner turned his attention to Viola, to Bill. Her with her eyes hidden behind those dark hipster shades. Him with his hard and fast stare.

There was a generation of emotions looking back at that attorney.

"The snapshot shouts out, doesn't it," said Viola.

Gardner set the snapshot down on the dashboard.

Up ahead was a diner. Bill pointed to it. "We have time," he said. "Let's stop there... Have a Last Supper sort of thing... Before we do the face off."

"That's not funny," said Viola, slapping the back of his head.

Then she leaned forward and got right in behind Bill. She kissed two fingers and touched his cheek scar like that day all those years ago in the baby blue Lincoln.

Bill checked her out in the rearview. Offered her a look of unquestionable affection.

Bill pulled into the diner parking lot.

Gardner went from watching those two to glancing at the snapshot. The sun through the front window making the letters almost burn:

America v. America
Outcome Uncertain